TERESA M. ASH

RESCUE IN TIME 2

STARTING AGAIN

ISBN
978-1-963254-64-8 (Paperback)
978-1-963254-65-5 (eBook)

RESCUE IN TIME

STARTING AGAIN

TABLE OF CONTENTS

THEME

The Interplanetary Council of Diplomats (ICD) has chosen Earth as their next planet to explore and hopes to form diplomatic relations. The Council hopes to find a planet where goodness rules and, thus causing a productive worldwide community to form. The Council intends to send their best representatives as scouts to the planet and determine whether the inhabitants are worthy of saving or not.

Meanwhile, another faction of aliens intends to destroy all the earth's inhabitants and to use the resources for personal gain. The last thing they want is for the Council to gain strength through the goodness of the inhabitants of another planet.

INTRODUCTION

The leading character, Tom Clancey, thought his grandfather was simply a senile old man living out his last days in some sort of fantasy, until, on Tom's 21st birthday, his grandfather reveals a secret hidden in his most treasured possession, an antique clock. Tom is stunned when the clock reveals that his grandfather is the only living soul on earth entrusted to be the point of contact and ambassador to visitors from distant worlds. He is equally amazed to discover that the mantle has been passed down to him instead of his father.

Now at 28, and on his own, equipping these visitors to adapt to earth in his one-bedroom apartment is a major challenge. The amazing adventures began when the 12-inch alien was taken by a thief. The adventures in book 2 continue when the dragon-like alien is swept away by the Colorado Rapids. His dragon-like mate pursues after him and ends up being swept away as well. It does not take Tom too long to conclude that the rigid lizard textured skin of two of the visitors is not make-up. To his amazement, Cally, the shapeshifter is not the only one with hidden powers. The lizard creatures take flight to hunt their next meal and raise havoc someplace they were not supposed to be.

PRELUDE

They represent a total of 9 planets located in three universes spread throughout the Nubian Sea Galaxy. However, only three species are to be selected to make first contact with the most primitive species known to them all as humans.

The Interplanetary Council members consist of the following:

The Tarianas are olive green, khaki tan, and yellow. They slither on their bellies like cobras reared back for an attack and are the size of full-grown 6-foot-tall human beings.

The Nubians have giraffe-like necks and colorful male peacock feathered tails. Below the torso they have two lanky legs. But unlike most creatures, below the waist they only have two long lanky legs and no visible waistlines.

The Mawtojwas (má-tá-was) have the appearance of pure crystal blue liquid. They must remain in liquid stasis most of the time in order to avoid contamination. The liquid flows in and out of itself like the flow water at a crossroad. The waters also constantly emanate low pulses of ocean blue light. These creatures emerged out of the Eridanus constellation as well. They are from the Cypress Moon.

The Crustaceans are small elf-like creatures with large cranial foreheads. These foreheads are seldom seen since an upside-down bowl-shape covering is worn for protection. They are from the planet Sedna. This planet is within the Kuiper Belt.

The Junipahs are creatures of light. Their appearance is that of brilliant rainbow shimmering lights. Whenever they encounter other species, they encase themselves within gold metallic suits. They dwell on the planet Amplicus which is 3.5 times larger than Earth and 352 light years away.

The Lopus is one of the life forms selected to be ambassador to earth by the ICD. The Lopus resides somewhere within the Nubian galaxy, however, no one knows exactly where. This Lopus was chosen because of its' ability to take on any form it chooses; its' kinetic abilities; and its' multi-linguistic talents. It is capable of being understood in more than a thousand languages simultaneously. No one, apart from their parent, really knows their identity and on this occasion, it will assume a human female form.

The Lizaradactiles have been selected to accompany the Lopus on the journey to earth. These creatures, from the planet Prehistoria, are located 600 light-years away from the Kuiper Belt. They have bodies that closely resemble dragons. With skin as tough as nails, they can withstand the full force of any human handheld projectile weapon. The ICD noted that their uncommon strength would be useful to the team. Therefore, the ICD unanimously agrees they will make the best bodyguards. And since they are the height and size of the average human being, they can easily be camouflaged.

The Rumerangues mostly reside on Aquarian, a planet located on the outer realm of the Nubian Galaxy. Their society leaders insisted that their representative be allowed to visit earth along with the other ambassadors. They reasoned that their technological advancements in information gathering sets them apart from all other participants. The problem the ICD members have with this species is that they are only 15 inches or so in height. For the most part, their appearance is that of a human. They argue that their flattened foreheads, shaped by alligator-type ridges in the center, are hardly even noticeable. Nevertheless, to have their demands met, the Rumerangue had to agree to surgically alter the forehead to resemble that of a human's. He also is expected to assume the role of a human doll unless otherwise needed.

The ICD of aliens meet on Venus at least once every full planet rotation to discuss improving their sectors. This meeting, however, is about sending a group of scouts to earth to save it from total annihilation.

CHAPTER 1

NOSY NEIGHBOR

Bernard Stevens, an English Professor at The University of Denver, is startled by noise coming from the hallway. He springs to his feet, almost tripping over them, while making his way to the door. The Professor peeps through the peephole and notices an attractive, brown-skinned woman carrying over-stuffed bags of groceries. Bernard was told by his neighbor, Tom Clancey, that friends would be staying with him for a short while. Thin hands tuck a green and black paisley pajama shirt into a baggy pajama bottom. This thoughtful gift from his mother is his favorite pair of pajamas. Everything she buys for him is a size too large though. She still sees Bernard as being that chubby little boy in sixth grade.

The Professor notices Tom carrying bags too. He normally would've minded his own business, but, since Tom has been such a good neighbor, he mustards up enough courage to open his door. The Professor is the nervous type and a bit like Jim Carrey's comical side. He stumbles into the hallway and reaches for a bag about to slip out of Tom's hands. "Ugh… Allow me," he says.

The bag topples over onto the Professor's chest. At the same time, Tom fumbles through his collection of keys until he finds the one that fits the lock.

Thanks Professor, I have it," he assures him.

"You have it, so, why are you still out of breath?" The Professor commands the keys and opens the door before Tom has a chance to refuse his services. To his surprise, on the other side of the door is a creature unlike anything he has ever seen before. It appears to be grazing on the floor like a cow. Its skin has the appearance of a lizard, and its head is twice the size of a normal human.

"Hi Mr. Bernie!" greets Terry who is busy searching for food under the sofa cushions. She had seen him walking to the bus stop and even spied on him by peeping through his bedroom window a few times. She feels like she knows him now, even though she doesn't.

Her salutation leaves the Professor totally dumbfounded and wondering how she knows him. Her speech is eloquent, yet her appearance is like something out of a sci-fi movie.

Despite Tom's attempts to excuse the Professor at the door, Bernie has other plans. He forces his way into the kitchen.

Meanwhile, Cally trails behind them both with more bags of groceries. She quickly surveys the situation and determines that the Professor is a threat who must be eliminated. Through Extra Sensory Perception (ESP) Cally knows the Professor intends to tell all he has seen. Without delay, he closes in on Tom, who races down the flight of stairs to gather the remaining groceries.

"Thanks for your help, Professor. I can handle it from here, really, I can," Tom respectfully reassures him.

"Allow me," the Profession persists. "And please…" he pauses. "Call me Bernie." The Professor carries the bags into the kitchen. "I just have one question."

"Okay. What is it?" Tom allows.

This had better be good, the Professor thinks while carefully crafting his question. Tom knows I love acting and going to the theater too, so, how could he expect to keep this from me?

"Why the costumes and what play are they rehearsing for?" Tom turns his head to avoid the Professor's discerning gaze.

"It's a long story. I'll explain it to you over coffee someday, but not today. Be a sport, won't you?" Tom appeases while gently pushing the Professor towards the door.

"I'm not having a good day today," Tom says apologetically.

"Good night Mr. Bernie!" yells Terry across the hall. She watches the Professor close his door.

Cally limps into the living room and plops down on the sofa next to G. W. who has just come out of hiding. Tom stops all he is doing when he hears her moaning in pain. He gently places her leg over his and takes a closer look at the calve.

"It's swollen to double in size and is red as a beet." He whistles. "I can't believe you allowed yourself to be dragged out tonight with this ankle. What were you thinking?" he wonders. Cally never shared how she got this wound. While Frank and Terry hid in a tree, she climbed into the window of the house where G. W. was held a prisoner. Without warning, a vicious dog came out of nowhere and bit her leg. Cally immediately turned into a black panther and frightened the dog away. Cally kept this part of the rescue to herself because she believed she would be healed by now.

"You need ice on that ankle," Tom tells her. "You should have told me about this sooner instead of going to the store like you did."

"I thought you needed help. My body usually self-heals," she assures while flinching from pain.

Frank and Terry get to eat again and this time they wolf down two roasted chickens and two super-sized bags of potato chips.

Tom is much too exhausted from shopping to eat, so he retreats to his bedroom. Before falling asleep, he makes a mental note to never forget to double stock his pantry so long as these Aliens are on Earth.

Cally's pain is sharp and throbbing, even to the point of bringing tears to her eyes. She is amazed at how fragile the human body really is. Nevertheless, she is determined to stay focused on all that needs to be done. A sudden sense of urgency brings the Professor to mind.

"I believe he can use a mint," she says aloud while limping across the hall to his place.

The Professor hears a faint knock at his door. He sighs while getting out of his comfortable recliner. "Who can this be?" he wonders while looking through the peephole. The Professor is thrilled to see Cally. He pushed a head full of pepper grayed hair back with one hand and opens the door with the other.

"Awe! Cally! It is always a pleasure to see your lovely face. What can I do for you?" he wonders.

She extends a hand towards him and opens a clinched fist. Inside her hand is a florescent royal blue mint wrapped in plastic wrapper.

"We all would like for you to try this new cool mint. It's our way of saying thanks for helping with the groceries," she explains.

He takes the mint out of her hand, bows, then, graciously thanks her for it.

"Wait a minute!" she says while pushing against the closing door. "I'd like to see you enjoy it in my presence, please-e-e," she cunningly purrs.

He pops the glistening mint into his mouth. It lands on his tongue and slowly melts. It leaves him with the sensation of sweet cherry Italian ice.

Suddenly, he is whisked away into his childhood, when he was merely eight years old, to be exact. This was the year his father returned from the Desert Storm War and the happiest moment of his childhood. Everyone else was sad since his father had been severely wounded and medically discharged from the Air Force. He, however, was happy because he was finally able to spend time with him.

Then, the scene changes, and he is back in high school, a week before the prom. He had just broken his leg playing football and would lose his football scholarship. This also meant he would not be able to attend the prom. Everyone else felt bad for him, but it was his happiest moment in High School. You see, he hated football. He only played football to please his father and he dreaded having to take the one cheerleader to the prom that had previously dated every guy on the team.

The scene changes once more, and he finds himself giving a speech to hundreds of students at Xavier University. He was the valedictorian of his class and had become what he longed to be all his life, a teacher. His mother and father led the standing ovation with tears in their eyes and admiration in their hearts. Suddenly, the journey through time comes to an end and the Professor finds himself reclining in his favorite chair watching a blaring TV.

"That was a pleasant and refreshing dream," he says aloud, but he is totally puzzled about how he spent his day. Everything is a big blur.

CHAPTER 2

GOING CAMPING

Frank struggles to loosen his seatbelt while in the back seat of the rented Camper. His pouting gets on Tom's nerves, even so, he puts up with it for the sake of the mission.

"For the tenth time," Tom explains. "Wearing seatbelts is the law and we must abide by the laws on Earth or else."

"Or else what…?" Frank groans. "I can't stand this thing any longer!" Frank tugs and pulls at his seatbelt to loosen it from across his broad chest.

"I agree… These things suck!" Terry adds before unbuckling her seatbelt as well. She slides over next to her partner.

"If only we could settle in the back," Frank whispers, and then, winks his double-layered eyelids, which always signifies that he wants a favor from his spouse.

"Please…" he begs while wishing that Terry will be his spokesperson. He believes she'll resolve this issue for them once and for all since Tom gives in to his wife more than him.

"Tom?" she says in a soft voice. "I have a request to make of you…" her voice quivers before it pauses.

"I would like…" she pauses again.

"We would like…" Frank abruptly interrupts.

"We have a request," she continues. "We-e-e would like to spend the rest of our trip in the back. These restraints are much too uncomfortable for us." She glances at Frank who quickly gives a nod of approval.

Tom glances over at Cally for her opinion on the matter.

"What do you think?" he asks Cally.

"Would you like to carry two sleeping Lizaradactiles once we get to our campsite?" she responds.

Tom looks back at Terry through his rear-view mirror.

"Hang on," he tells them. "We're almost there. The sun will be up soon, and I intend to cook a big meal just before you two fall asleep."

They had to leave Denver early that morning, long before dawn, just so the Lizaradactiles, being the nocturnal creatures they are, would be ready to sleep once they arrived at the campsite.

As much as Tom has tried to get along with them, they still leave him with an unsettling feeling deep within the pit of his stomach. He wishes he had the built-in defense mechanism Cally enjoys, then, he could change himself into something huge and menacing whenever they threaten his well-being. Tom hopes he packed enough meat for them all. He believes he did pack enough food, even so, that nagging doubt just won't go away.

"Almost there," he assures everyone again. "And the sun coming up will give us just enough light to put the tents up too."

G. W. silently sits in the back on the dollhouse chair which Tom turned into a safety seat just for him. It is surrounded by utility netting, is equipped with a safety belt, and is positioned at the rear of the van.

Streaks of daylight invade G. W.'s space and piques his curiosity. What lies beyond this primitive machine, he wonders? G. W. daringly climbs out of the safety seat. Tiny hands reach up to grab hold of the cord dangling next to the blinds. With all his strength, he tugs on the cord. Without warning, the weight of his body causes the entire blinds to rise. The littlest alien holds tight onto the cord and propels to the floor.

Rays of light shine on dew covered meadows and dance off unsuspecting Aspen trees. Like the magic created by the turning of a kaleidoscope, the big sky mountain range slowly transforms the black of night into vivid purples, orange-reds, yellow-golds, then, back to orange again. Being enamored by the view, he nearly forgets to create visual recordings of all the beauty surrounding him. This Rumerangue has come fully equipped with an endless capacity memory bank. This has been a well-kept secret for centuries by his species. Also, their small size is a plus because it enables them to get in and out of most places undetected. Their ability to pose as sentient beings and conceal the fact that they are an artificial life form, a robot in some cultures, is a secret the Rumerangues intend to conceal forever.

More than a millennium ago a deadly plague nearly wiped out their entire civilization. The few remaining scientists knew they had to come up with a plan that would keep their civilization alive. So, they created an artificial life form a fraction of their original size who could house their consciousness. The purpose for this creation is to enable them to invade the privacy of others whenever it is deemed necessary. Their brains can store an endless amount of data. Their bodies are capable of digesting vegetables and other light foods to give the appearance that they are organic. And all these artificial life forms have a built-in defense mechanism capable of destroying the least to the greatest of life forms on planet Earth.

G. W. is anxious to explore more of this planet and day-by-day is growing fonder of the humans. Also, he is becoming more and more apprehensive about betraying every life form on this primitive world simply to satisfy an old family debt. Yes, his family is indebted to the dastardly league of rebels plotting against this mission.

Tom eases the van into a half-empty parking lot and finds a parking spot leaving plenty of room on either side of it. His passengers exit the van one-by-one and stretch their legs while reaching for the sky. While Tom unloads the camping gear and food from the back, Frank and Terry are already discovering where civilization meets forest.

"Whoa! Guys! Don't go too far!" Tom commands. Their goal is to find something edible, and Frank believes anything will do.

Terry giggles as a chipmunk scurries over her feet.

"What's so funny?" Frank wonders in a souring tone. "I could've had that for a snack!"

"Have you seen G. W. lately?" she burst into laughter again.

"I wonder how Tom and Cally will react to G. W. being missing again," he wonders. "I guess one of us needs to speak up," he jokes.

"Well, I suppose we can both tell them that he's missing again." They both roar into laughter. Tom and Cally are still unloading camping gear when Frank tells them the bleak news.

"He's not lost. G. W. is in the back of the van," Cally replies in response to their news.

Frank drops the camping gear at the sight of a half-dollar sized spider. It scurries across the dirt-covered picnic table right into his hand. He positions it between two forefingers and pops it into his mouth.

"Yuk!" Tom shrieks at the sight of the kill.

Cally retrieves G. W. from the van on their last trip to unload it. He fusses and snipes at her for closing the door on him one-time too many.

"How would you like to be shut up in a furnace? That's right, it felt like I was locked inside a furnace!" he grips.

Tom pushes aside every other task to focus on building tents for Frank and Terry to sleep in. I have questions that need to be answered, he thinks, and maybe Cally can shed some light on a few things for me.

The largest tent is equipped with two sturdy closets that are perfect for Frank and Terry to sleep in. Tom gives them a dozen Italian sub sandwiches and then, invites the Lizaradactiles into their temporary abodes. Tom wants to lock them both in, but Cally insists that would be a huge mistake. "Why the sudden fear?" she wonders.

"I'm not sure," he answers. "It's just a feeling. Have I been told the whole truth about them? I mean" He pauses to find the right words.

"I saw Frank grab a big rutty spider and eat it like it was candy. Doesn't that just gross you out?" he winces.

She stops cold on the trail and gives him a curious look. Her warm brown eyes put him at ease, and he senses from her stare that there is nothing to worry about.

"I know you mean well by sharing this with me, but we're all different. We're all aliens, as you call it. I'm the first to admit that Frank and Terry are difficult to control because of their veracious appetites. Even so, that is just part of who they are. I know what you're afraid of. You fear they may turn to humans for food. I won't lie to you, if you happened to be on their planet, you would be the hunted delicacy. However, they are diplomats. They wear that title proudly and I am certain, no, positive that they won't betray your trust."

Suddenly, the expression on his face changes from pleasant to total horror. His heart is racing, and it has something to do with her face.

"What is it?" she demands as Tom points at her face. "Tell me!" she shouts.

He takes a step back away from her.

"Your face," he shudders. "It's falling apart."

Gaps appear between her eyes and nose, revealing nothing. Empty space is all that fills the gaps, and the same phenomenon is occurring to her hands. The flesh between each finger slowly disappears right before his frightened eyes.

"It's nothing to worry about," she calmly assures while pushing everything back together again. "I just need to regenerate this body. That's all."

Tom is somewhat relieved, yet, still shaken-up just the same.

"You mean sleep?" he questions.

"Yes," she answers. "That's all I need."

Tom rushes her back to the camp. "You…Me…And G. W. will sleep in this tent," he instructs while unzipping the Igloo shaped structure.

There's a hammock strung up in the far-right corner of the tent that gently sways from cool breezes blowing in from the entrance. "This is your bed," he shows her with a slight bow and wave of a hand.

"Just get to know them before you judge," she suggests through a drawn-out yawn.

Now, he realizes that not trusting Frank and Terry is out of line. Tom reminds himself that if anyone knows the tendencies of the Lizaradactiles—she does.

Seconds later, she is sound asleep, leaving Tom and G. W. alone in the tent.

"I've got an idea," suggests G. W. "Let's hit the trail. I'm sure we can make it back in time for their next feeding." Tom lowers his backpack to the ground.

"Climb aboard," he orders. G. W. climbs into the outer pouch, totally ready to explore the wilderness of planet Earth.

CHAPTER 3

NEW FOUND FRIEND

Tom heads due west, away from their campsite and deeper into unsettled territory. To ease his uncertainty, he chooses a trail leading a straight path back to their camp. He desperately wishes Cally could've joined them and suddenly realizes just how much her very presence brings him comfort. She's like the rock of Gibraltar standing strong and tall amid confusion.

"Those are pine trees," he explains while pointing to a nearby cluster. Tom is determined to name as many trees as possible for the littlest alien who is dutifully storing all this information into his vast memory bank.

"What's that," G. W. wonders. "Look to your right," he directs. Tom looks just in time to see a 5-point mule deer and quickly reaches for his phone.

"Excuse me my friend, that is the best of the deer family," he proudly proclaims as though he had something directly to do with it. "I need to take a picture of this baby."

The flash from his camera phone startles the deer. It causes it to dart into the nearby foliage, well-hidden from Tom's lens.

"Don't put your camera away yet," says G. W. "You're going to be so pleased when you see what I've just spotted."

Tom makes a 180-degree turn.

"I give up," he wonders "Where is it?"

He doubts that G. W. really can make a realistic call for his photo gallery. Nevertheless, Tom plays along and scans the forest for any more signs of wildlife. G. W. clears his throat.

"It's getting closer…" he announces, toying with Tom. "I believe you humans would say it is furry."

Tom becomes impatient and stomps his foot in protest.

"Okay, enough of this game. Where is the darn thing?" he demands.

G. W. finally reveals the creature's whereabouts.

"Look to your far left," he instructs.

Tom is at a loss for words because standing 50 feet away from him is the biggest and meanest looking grizzly he has ever laid eyes on. The 10-foot monstrosity sniffs the air while standing on its hind legs. It sees Tom, senses his fear, then, spews out a menacing roar. Without warning, it plants all four paws onto the ground and charges towards Tom. Its mouth quivers and foams with saliva. His roaring echoes through the trees, causing birds to flutter and take flight into the air. Tom's attempts to move become futile. Fear has him pinned down and frozen where he stands. His motionless body reeks with fear, then, his body takes refuge by rolling to its side and curling into the fetal position.

"Uh--Oh!" warns G. W. "I don't think it likes us."

Suddenly, a bear cub playfully waddles to the grizzly's side. Obviously, they've entered the nesting area of its apparent mother. She voices her displeasure with another menacing roar which vibrates the air around them. The little cub retreats into the forest and more than ever, Tom wishes for Cally. He is certain she could turn into something fiercer and would surely knock this grizzly clear out of the forest. He wonders whether G. W. realizes there is no reasoning with a creature like this. However, he does recall Cally mentioning that they all came equipped with some sort of intuitive defense mechanism. He has yet to see any signs of such a mechanism from G. W.

"Where is it?" Tom shrieks while the grizzly edges closer.

"What are you doing?" G. W. snarls.

"I'm assuming a position of submission. This just may prevent an attack," Tom quivers.

G. W. leaps out of the backpack.

"Attack?" he squeals. "I thought you were going to take a picture!"

G. W. rests his hands on his hips and takes a long, lingering look at the rapidly approaching adversary.

"So, that would explain all of the roaring," he muses.

Before Tom can figure out what he has planned, G. W. takes swift strides towards the grizzly and positions himself at an equal distance between the creature and Tom. The grizzly stops out of curiosity, all the while, sniffing the air around the tiny figure. It becomes immediately apparent that G. W. has angered him even more. As soon as the grizzly lunges forward to attack, G. W. spins around like a spinning top. He spins so fast that all anyone can see is a whirlwind of dust. The grizzly takes a few steps backwards and rears her head around in confusion over the spinning.

All the while, Tom remains in his submissive fetal position with eyes shut tight. A swift death would be good, he thinks, and prays for God to make it so. He can hear the beast panting with every ground-shaking stride. Tom draws in a deep breath in anticipation of its rage. The impending doom doesn't occur. Moments go by, so, he cracks one eye open to see what's going on. There, in the middle of nowhere, appears to be a spinning top. Next to this spinning apparatus is what appears to be some sort of thermal energy wall. This wall prevents the grizzly from getting to Tom. A stunned grizzly lay on its side. It is not moving, yet its chest slowly moves in and out. While easing his way towards the spinning object, Tom reaches into the backpack for G. W. and is surprised he is not there.

"G. W.?" he yells while peering down at the top. It slows in velocity. Suddenly, to Tom's surprise, it becomes clear that it is G. W.

"I had no idea," Tom sighs. "You don't need our protection. We need yours," he laughs.

G. W. gives Tom a curious look.

"Exactly," he confirms in a matter-of-fact manner. Tom glances back at the force-field and, with confidence, walks away.

"How long will that last?" he wonders.

"As long as it needs to," G. W. responds. "Yes… as long as it needs to my friend."

The trek back to camp is uneventful and in silence. Tom is amazed that the littlest alien saved him from the jaws of a grizzly. He believes G. W. is full of surprises and wonders what else he can do. Tom hopes Cally will shed light on any more of G. W.'s abilities.

Back at the camp, Tom finds Cally still fast asleep. He checks on Frank and Terry, and they too are sleeping peacefully.

"It's time to cook dinner," Tom tells G. W. "Care to help?"

"I'll gather wood for the pit fire," he volunteers.

Tom walks 50 paces away from the main camp area and selects a flat safe area for digging a fire pit.

Tom and G. W. dug a large pit and built a blazing fire in it. Tom lines it with rocks and adds lots of wood, twigs, and charcoal. Then he tops it off with a generous amount of lighter fluid.

He and G. W. toss foil wrapped meat, potatoes, and corn into the pit before covering it with dirt.

"Now this fire should burn for hours," he tells G. W. while walking back towards the campsite.

"Now this is what I call a barbecue," boasts Tom while pounding his fists against his chest like Tarzan.

Embers escape into the sky as Tom and his newfound friend rest near the fire. Tom thinks about the way G. W. rescues him from the grizzly. He was paralyzed by fear and wished for Cally, yet his hero was with him all along. The corners of his mouth roll up into a satisfying grin while glancing down at G. W. who stands brushing dirt off his clothes. The littlest alien pauses, looks up at Tom, then gingerly returns the smile.

CHAPTER 4

MYSTERIOUS WOOD PILE

The shadows of night creep over the camp while locusts and frogs serenade all who have ears to hear. An owl's hoot and a wolf's howl acknowledge the reign of night.

Tom's hopeful that Cally will wake up soon. He tip-toes into her tent to gaze upon her peacefully resting body.

"Awake…Awake," he whispers while hoping she'll wake up to help him with the Lizaradactiles. A sudden twitching of her foot causes him to step back and trip over her backpack. He falls on his butt, then promptly scrambles to his feet only to find Cally still sleeping soundly.

"If only you would wake up!" he pouts while leaving her tent. "I need you."

The sun has completely gone down over the horizon and the cool mountain air brings shivers up his spine. He steps over to the fire and pokes at it with a fallen branch. Embers sail through the air and shoot upwards, like fireflies, towards the sky. The ground is damp and hard beneath him. So, he stands to his feet and stretches towards the silvery moonlight. As he lifts an arm towards the deep blue sky, he is startled by the sound of someone or something approaching the camp.

"Who's there!" he calls while picking up a stick from the ground around the fire. A flashlight is only an arms-length away, so, Tom picks it up and shines it at the approaching targets.

"It's us!" yells Terry while waddling towards him from the forest.

Frank appears out of the thickets after her and is not as pleasant. "When do we eat?" he wants to know. His voice is loud and brusque and intimidating to Tom.

"Been up for long?" Tom wonders, all the while, attempting to conceal his fear.

"Not long," Terry answers and begins to rub her belly with both hands.

"It's time for us to eat though."

Frank nods in agreement.

They don't have to tell him twice. Tom scurries to the barbecue pit and digs up the foil wrapped vegetables, potatoes, and meats that have been smoldering for most of the day. They eat their fill and to Tom's amazement, Frank and Terry have had enough.

"No more for me," Frank tells him and ends his sentence with a loud lingering burp.

"I could use a walk," announces Terry while doing hand-over-head stretches. "I enjoyed those walks through the city when we searched for G. W. Speaking of G. W., where is he?" she wonders aloud.

"He's around here somewhere," Tom assures her. "He's too responsible to simply leave the camp on his own," he reasons and expects her to take his word for it.

"He's around here somewhere?" she mocks. "How can you be so casual about it?" she scolds. "Is anyone the least bit concerned?"

She stomps off towards G. W.'s tent and calls out his name.

"G. W., are you in here?"

She listens for an answer, then, proceeds by rummaging through his backpack and probing his tiny sleeping bag.

"I'm off to the woods," Terry announces to the men lounging beside the warmth of the campfire. "Would anyone care to join me?" she beckons while inching backwards into the forest.

"Hey G. W., are you there?" she calls into the darkness and far away from the warmth and light of the flames.

"I guess G. W. must have wandered off again. I can't seem to find him anywhere."

She twirls around and stares in their direction. Terry hopes that at least one of them will join her.

G. W. being lost again is highly unlikely as far as Tom is concerned. He has seen the little fellow in action and is confident that he can take care of himself out here in the wild.

"I didn't realize he was lost!" Tom cracks. She catches the irritation in his voice. He doesn't want to be reminded of the last fiasco when he left G. W. unattended in a public place. His little visitor was snatched, kidnapped, mistaken for a doll, and almost bitten by a spider and it was entirely his fault. He felt he'd let everyone down, especially his grandfather, and wonders if the same bad luck could strike again so soon.

"You tell me you're not serious. This is a joke, right?" he complains while standing to his feet.

"No joke Tom, I am very serious," she answers without hesitation.

"If you're right..." Tom fears while leaping to his feet. "We need to search every nook and cranny. Don't leave any place untouched," he panics. "He must be around here somewhere. And we're going to find him tonight!"

Tom leaves the comfort of the campfire to join Terry in the search for his little friend. He pulls out every bag, opens every container, and then, turns over every pot, pan, plate, and saucer in the camp.

Frank doesn't feel like investing time or energy in another search for G. W. and sneers as Terry gives him 'the look'. This look is like the stare a mother gives a mischievous child out in public.

"Okay! I'll help if this means you'll stop worrying me to death," he pouts then slowly struggles to his feet.

He recalls losing himself once as a little tot. His father was so distraught about it, he missed the hunt of the century. Hunting is the driving-force behind his species and the more dangerous the hunt, the better. He has never forgiven himself for causing his father to miss that hunt, even though his father never expressed a bit of remorse against him.

Suddenly, a gush of chilly autumn wind blows leaves into the camp. Terry looks behind her and stares deep into the dark forest.

"Did you hear that?" Terry asks after hearing a distinct crackling of twigs nearby. Without considering the danger, she follows the sound into the dark forest.

"Terry jumps at every little thing," Frank scoffs.

Even so, Tom comes to attention as well and has a hunch not to ignore her premonition.

"She gets this way sometimes," Frank smirks, then, quickly backs off the moment Tom's calm expression changes into a troubled creased forehead worry. Frank is certain he knows what may come next. He suspects there will be a pursuit into the dark woods. Frank is certain that if he doesn't come along, he'll be branded as the one who didn't care enough about another team member.

Sure enough, Tom does insist on everyone leaving the comfort of the fire to venture into the forest in search of G. W. Terry agrees wholeheartedly, and their decision leaves Frank outnumbered two-to-one.

Leaves fly into the air when he kicks the ground in frustration. Tom and Terry take off in the direction of the sound. Frank trails behind.

"Hey!" Frank stresses. "You two do know we're going to need more nourishment after the search." Neither Tom nor Terry pays any attention to his comment. They march ahead into the darkness until Frank loses sight of them.

"Hey guys, wait up!" he calls and is forced to run and skip to catch up.

Back at the camp, Cally rolls over onto her back and struggles to open her eyes. A flood of emotions invades her mind and sound an alarm deep within the inner man. Weary eyes pop open when she senses that something is wrong within the camp. She tells herself that she must get up to help and attempts to do so. For the first time in her life, she felt the weight of her legs. They shake as she heaves them to one side of the hammock. She eases her body down to the ground and, to Cally's surprise, her legs refuse to stand up for long. She takes one small step forward and topples down onto the ground. Luckily, she's still in arms reach of the hammock and uses the strength of her upper body to pull herself back onto it. While sitting on the edge of the hammock, she senses the life of the forest in greater depth than before. Cally is now keenly aware of the longings of an owl, the fearful heart of a lone deer and the racing heart of a hiding hare. The rejuvenation is a success. She senses a snake invading a gopher's den, a wolf pack gathering for a midnight howl at the moon, and moths spinning their cocoons.

"I must make my way to my friends," she says aloud. "G. W. is okay."

Away from the camp and deep within the forest, Tom, Terry, and Frank continue to search for G. W. Suddenly, Terry is startled by a pile of logs that appear to be floating towards her.

"It's, it's, well, it's floating!" she screams in alarm. "Ooh! What's that?" she points. "Nobody ever told me there would be creatures made of wood on this planet!" she shouts while running back into the arms of Frank.

Frank is not afraid of the so-called, floating pile of wood. He keeps a watchful eye on it as it moves closer towards them. Tom's not afraid of it either and motions for them to follow him as he follows it.

"Let's take a closer look. Follow it. We'll see where it leads us," he suggests.

No one even notices Cally. She gracefully waltzes towards the pile of hovering wood.

"I could use a little help!" shouts G. W.

"You look like you can handle it all by yourself," Cally responds with a refreshing smile. Then, she takes several logs off the stack G. W. is carrying.

"Look! Look! There's Cally!" shrieks Terry. "What on earth are you doing here?" she wonders.

"Yeah," Frank says like he's disappointed about seeing her. "She means, seeing you is a surprise."

Seeing Cally is an unwelcome site for Frank and Terry and they both groan in protest. She'll put a wrench on our plans for sure, thinks Frank. With her on the scene again, he pouts, it'll be difficult, very difficult for us to slip away on our own. He assures himself though that somehow, they will come up with a way to explore on their own.

"I know what you both mean," she responds while shrugging her shoulders and turning towards Tom. "It doesn't matter."

"Tom," she smiles while walking towards him. "It's good to be up again."

"I thought we wouldn't see you up on your feet again until tomorrow this time," he says and welcomes her with open arms and a kiss on the cheek.

"Evidently, I'm needed," she says while squeezing him closer to warm her body. Tom steps back and still holds on to her. He feels a little melancholy while thinking about how sad he will be to see her go once their mission ends on earth.

G. W. passes by with an arm full of wood. He balances more than a foot of wood on his thin arms.

"Hold on little buddy," Tom tells him. "You shouldn't have to do this all by yourself."

Tom takes the stack of wood out of his arms and tosses them onto the fire. Then, he heads back into the forest for more wood. The others follow Tom and gather wood for the fire as well.

"We'll need a lot more wood for reserve," he lets them know. "I'll need to start cooking soon."

"Frankly…" pauses Frank. "I'm a bit surprised G. W. has this much strength," he sighs while gathering more wood. He always thought that the only value this little creature had was as a snack between meals. He admits to himself that he was wrong to presume another person's weaknesses and worth. This is one of the first rules of engagement in the wild: Don't presume anything or else you may lose your life to the prey.

"Next time, take one of us with you on your back woods excursions," scolds Cally. "You could have been injured."

"Or even worse…" she warns. "You may have been eaten!"

If they only knew, thinks Tom, if they only knew the value of this man; this creature; this machine. He can take care of himself and mustn't be treated like a child; no; not anymore. He crouches down on one knee next to G. W. to express his gratitude face-to-face.

"Thank you, my friend," he sincerely tells him. "I really appreciate this. I'd forgotten all about the wood. It's a good thing you're here to help," he says while lifting the last piece of wood from the littlest alien's hands and tossing it onto the flames. The fire crackles and leaps in appreciation of being fed.

CHAPTER 5

DISCOVERY

With legs crossed Indian-style, Cally relaxes on the hammock in hopes of recovering her equilibrium soon. Her senses, however, are sharper than ever. Therefore, she is not surprised when Tom enters her tent.

"I apologize for the intrusion. Got a minute or two?" he asks while easing down next to her on the hammock.

Cally stares deep into his ocean blue eyes and discerns every thought.

"Is there anything wrong? Care to share?" she asks, even though the question is already known to her.

"What would you like to know?" she asks now dandling both feet over one side of the hammock.

"I'm ready to hear all you know about G. W.," she tells him.

He rears back in amazement.

"I never said anything about G. W.," he gulps in a breath of air to calm his nerves.

"Sure, you did," she responds.

"No, I didn't," he assures her.

"Well, maybe I probed your thoughts a little," she confesses remorsefully.

Her intrusion has him on edge and he's tempted to walk out, but then, he decides to overlook it. He wants to tell her all about the incident involving G. W. and the grizzly. Cally's insight is invaluable and as the leader of the other aliens, he suspects she will know all about G. W.'s capabilities.

"To be honest about it, I saw the entire incident while I was asleep and it grieved me deeply," she explains. She knows that any attempt to conceal her knowledge of the incident will cause more friction and mistrust between them. "Even so, I had no idea that G. W. was capable of saving you or anyone else for that matter."

The truth spills out. It overflows into the atmosphere. It causes Cally to conclude that she has limitations. She is not able to read every creature's mind. Apparently, G. W. is no ordinary creature.

"You didn't know either?" Tom says in surprise. "Well, you can imagine the shock it was for me. That bear came out of nowhere and had it not been for him, I'd probably be dead right now."

Cally thinks back to the briefing they all received before coming to earth. The only thing she recalls about G. W.'s skills and capabilities is his ability to store data. Also, she does recall one Council member saying that G. W. can take care of himself. She peers up at Tom who just stood to his feet.

"I honestly believed he was all intellect," she confesses.

Her mind wanders back to the Interplanetary Council meeting:

It is called-to-order at "The Dawn of the New Day" stadium. This incredible stadium is suspended high above the universally diverse city of Nequada on Sedna within the Kuiper Belt and home world to the Crustaceous. Nine planet governments sent three ambassadors each to represent their interests at the council meeting. They gathered inside of the domed stadium under tight security. At this meeting, each representative was encased within a catacomb of metallic beams and glass, well-protected from the atmosphere and would-be assassins. The delegates and spectators alike all appeared to be seated in thin air throughout the massive structure. However, in all actuality, each seat was re-enforced with an electro-magnetic field designed to comfortably hold, surround, and protect every bodily frame and type imaginable. A measure of protection had to be implemented due to threats against those who pursue diplomatic relations with humans. Various populous throughout the many worlds believe that earth should be taken by force. They reason that those humans (who are among the most primitive of all species throughout the galaxy) should be used as chattels or slaves.

Conversely, the supporters of Ishi and Ishi himself, have forbidden such action. Ishi is the invisible ruler of planet Earth as well as the galaxies and worlds beyond. He is known by many names. Ishi is the name most frequently used throughout the world in existence. He is also respected by many societies and works side-by-side with the populous. And, in so doing, he has established advanced societies in technology and on the spiritual awareness level. Sprinkled throughout these worlds are a small band of renegades. These rebels have come together for the purpose of destroying all peaceful negotiations. At this moment, they are planning an attack against Earth.

Cally recalls how persistent the Rumerangue's Council member was at the meeting.

"I will not calm down until my demands are not only heard, but met," he passionately argued until everyone agreed to allow G. W. to visit earth as an ambassador.

Cally turns to Tom and tells him:

"This is worth further investigation."

She pulls both feet back onto the hammock and sits Indian style again.

"Meditation is needed," she explains while closing both eyes.

Tom quietly leaves her tent and can't help but notice the blanket of stars filling the dark Colorado sky. He tries to imagine how it would feel to visit at least one of those worlds and wonders what he would see or where he would go. One thing is for certain, he knows he'd miss friends and family. The way of life he has grown so accustomed to living would be gone. A shooting star streaks across the sky. Tom makes a wish concerning Laura. He wishes for her to love him as much as he loves her. Another star crosses his path. This time he prays for unity and peace among the Ambassadors. He also hopes, in the final analysis, nothing will ever put a strain on their relationship again. Instead of retiring to his tent, he decides to lounge next to the blazing fire. He wonders what dangers and adventures still lay ahead.

CHAPTER 6
DEADLY EXCURSION

Frank and Terry sneak into the forest and the harvest moon provides all the light they need. Even though they have eagle vision, they are thankful for the added illumination.

"The night is young," Terry whispers as they inch their way deeper and deeper into the abyss of the unknown. She intends to explore every inch of planet earth. Excitement over their clever plan to leave camp causes laughter to bubble up and overflow from within.

"Calm down and watch where you're going," Frank warns.

Her mate has hunted prey enough to know how to carefully maneuver in places like this and to keep himself out of harm's way. Terry, on the other hand, is so excited, she races through the forest without taking any precautions. Frank's mouth drools with anticipation of having a feast in the forest. He heard rumors about the abundance of fresh prey on earth. Now he has the chance to find out firsthand. Tom never mentions anything about hunting, not one word. Frank believes he would save Tom a lot of time and money if he was allowed to hunt for himself.

After a brisk 30-minute walk, they come to a clearing where the tall straw-like grass extends up to their waists. Frank extends his neck and sniffs in every direction for any signs of food.

He slaps a hand against his thigh and scowls, "Where is it? "I don't see or hear a single living creature."

Terry frowns, then snorts. She sniffs the air around them and doesn't sense any prey either. She marches ahead into the clearing and motions with one hand for Frank to follow. He does with a growl that frustrates her a little. She hates it when her mate gives up at the first sign of defeat.

"You know, there is more to life than your fat belly," she snaps while they traipse through the clearing towards the tree line ahead.

"Watch where you're going! There's a tree ahead!" he warns as they enter the forest again. "You dodo bird!" he shouts. Terry is startled into turning around just before walking into a huge tree.

"Tree!" she shrieks. "I thought we'd never reach the forest again."

"You almost backed into that tree and never-say-never," he snaps again. "Watch out!"

She narrowly misses another tree and stumbles over her own two feet. Frank topples over her and when the two of them butt their heads they're knocked senseless. Luckily for them, the mud, fresh leaves, and their exoskeletal shells cushion the fall.

"That was close," she giggles while drawing Frank into her bosom. They laugh and roll in the grass between two trees positioned only an arm's length apart. Then, without warning, she pushes him away and scrambles to her feet.

"What is it?" Frank wonders.

She sniffs the cool mountain air.

"I smell fish. Don't you?"

"Oh yeah," he replies.

"This way!" she marches while confidently allowing her nose to lead the way.

They march through the dense forest. The vegetation grows thicker, as the trail turns into a descending hill. They weave in and out of trees and shrubbery along a narrowing path. They leap over fallen tree limbs and tear through tightly woven shrubbery when, suddenly, the route becomes steeper. It becomes increasingly difficult to maintain control over their rapid descent. Even so, they don't attempt to slow down. The lust for fresh prey drives them to go faster. She sprints ahead of him. They sense the prey. They smell their next meal. Frank leaps to close the gap between them. He loses sight of her, then, regains it for an instant. Without warning, she drops out of view. He panics and calls out to her. She fails to answer. He forces his body to move even faster to catch up.

He calls out to her again, and then, without warning, discovers her fate firsthand. The earth beneath his feet becomes thin air. Before Frank has a chance to extend his wings, he descends downward and plunges into the frigid waters of the raging Colorado River rapids. The force of the water carries him down river, swiftly and without mercy, causing him to lose all sense of direction. Balky arms and muscular legs splash and push against the current. His lungs struggle for air as the weight of his densely boned structure forces his body further down beneath the raging white rapids. The spine-tingling waters invade the tightly woven layers of feathers against his skin. Frank loses buoyancy. His exhausted body sinks below the surface of the river. The deep claims him and rejoices in victory over another subject being added to its aquatic kingdom.

CHAPTER 7

THE GREAT FIND

Mat Crawford has given up all together on being accepted by the people of the mountain community of Crescent Butt, Colorado. The picturesque former mining town, with a total population of 1,487, takes great pride in making every tourist feel at home. He takes great pride in everything and everyone living in his adopted town. Mat is a big man according to everyone's standards. His enormous 6 feet 7 inches frame is daunting. And his long dark hair draped over his forehead, has earned him the nickname of "Bigfoot". He's grown to accept the label. Mat enjoys chasing the loopy-looks off of his 450-acre ranch.

"Cast your line over here," he yells to Amy, his new bride, while they fish on their private part of the lake.

Every morning before breakfast he takes her fishing at the river running through his property. The town's people were so taken aback by him marrying that someone spread the rumor he had bought a mail-order bride.

"Who in their right mind would marry a Bigfoot?" Gladys Connors said to her husband the moment she heard the news.

"Now, we mustn't say things like that Gladys," Jim Connors calmly advised. "It's always been said that there is someone for everyone. I married you, didn't I?" he slyly interjected while hiding behind his morning newspaper. She immediately shoots him a sinister look.

He thoroughly enjoys sticking pins and needles into his wife of 40 years. Their love runs deep, although she always has something derogatory to say about everyone they've ever encountered.

"Anyway," she sighs. "I saw his new bride, Amy, at the beauty parlor yesterday and she starts telling us ladies about how intelligent her husband is. Can you believe it? She wanted us to believe he graduated from Harvard and was number one in his class. Then, she invites us all over to her place to see… oh, how did she put it… The exquisite architectural designs her husband built into their home." Gladys licks her lips after taking a few quick sips of steaming hot coffee.

"So, are you going?" Jim calmly asks.

"Going where?" she snaps while practically dropping her coffee cup in her lap.

"Are you going to her house?" he earnestly inquires again. He is somewhat concerned by her lack of focus since just last week the doctor confided in him that his wife is in the early stages of dementia.

"Definitely not!" she hastily replies, leaving no room for doubt.

"Well, if you go, we can all find out if he is a good handyman or not," he says. "I need to find someone who can do some work around this old place."

"Hum…" she huffs while clanging a spoon against her empty cup.

Mat and Amy Crawford's cabin is positioned on a steep hill above a river. They both enjoy getting out into the open air and fishing at this river. This morning they used the well-worn trail behind their cabin to go down to the river to fish. Baiting the hook has always been a chore for Amy, but today she is determined to get the job done all by herself. She pricks a finger with the hook and turns to Mat for help.

"Ouch!" she whines.

The slippery fish bait drops to the sand one-time-too- many for her.

"Honey," she pouts while surrendering the rod and reel to her husband.

"I thought you'd never ask," he nods and grabs the tip of the pole, slides a new fish bait onto the hook, then, tosses the line into the water.

Moments later something gently nibbles at her bait. "Oops!" She screeches as the rod slightly bends towards the water. Mat jumps up and wedges his rod between two large rocks then races to rescue her rod.

"You're just lucky," he laughs while commandeering her rod and attempting to reel it to shore. He marvels at the fact that she always seems to snag a fish first, even though she doesn't consider fishing to be a sport or much fun.

"Let me show you how it's done," he beams. He is used to being in control. He not only graduated from Harvard as first in his Class, but he also retired from there as a professor. He met Amy there when she was a student. They dated in secret, and then, against the wishes of friends and family alike, they got married. They decided to relocate to someplace new for a fresh start. As a Biology Major, she was thrilled to be able to move to a place teaming with wildlife and the possibility of new biological discoveries every day. Thus, a great deal of her time is spent combing through forest lands for specimens and researching their origins in her home laboratory. Mat's confidence is one of the many attributes she admires most in him. So, even though she knows all about the art of fishing, she allows him the pleasure of teaching her all he knows and all she knows all over again.

He slowly reels in her catch and tugs a tad on the line to determine the weight of the fish. "This is a big one," he declares and pulls the line towards him with all his strength. It suddenly snaps and the bobber floats on top of the water. "That's odd," he observes while thinking that most freshwater fish would not have had the power to break a heavy line like that. This, he observes, usually happens during his deep-sea fishing trips.

"Could that big fish be caught on something?" she wonders after noticing that the fishing line has not moved since it snapped off and the bobber landed on top of the water.

Mat's head moves from side-to-side as he cautiously enters the water.

"Where are you going?" she demands while fearing he could be bitten by the enormous fish. "You could be killed!" she warns.

By now though, he has already entered the water and is tugging on string. He follows the line through shallow rushing waters toward a solid object. "This is no fish," he concludes.

He crouches in the water and brushes away the white foam created by the rapids. Now that he can see, his hands follow the line until they touch the actual object. He doesn't second guess his find and cautiously reaches down into the foaming frigid waters. The unexpected catch-of-the-day is a body. Even though Mat weighs well over 250 pounds and is a foot taller than most, he struggles to pull this poor soul out of the frigid Colorado rapids.

Amy is bewildered by the appearance of this victim. She has seen plenty of cadavers throughout her career, yet, she has never seen a decomposing body look like this before.

"Who is it? Or should I ask, what is it?" she wonders while attempting to pull the victim by the arm.

"Stay back," he insists. "You don't need to see this."

Mat plops the lifeless body down onto the beach.

"It's too late for caution," she tells him. "I've already seen the body and have decided to examine this one before the coroner gets here."

With one raised eyebrow she circles the body lying face-up at her feet. At closer examination, she begins to conclude, its abnormal appearance is not due to its demise. She notices the unusual width of its skull and the tight scale-like substance covering its skin. Eyelids and brows are nonexistent, and she notices that its skin has the clammy cold feel of a lizard with feathers. She takes a cautious step back.

"Let's get this creature away from the shore," he suggests. "We don't want our find to be swept away by the tide tonight."

Mat and Amy hope with all their might that this is a new discovery.

"Not by power…" he strains while pulling the creature further onto the bank. "Nor by might…" he declares and tugs even harder. "Dead weight," he moans. Amy grabs the creature's arm to ease Mat's heavy load. He quickly waves her away.

"Now Mat," she stops and stares at him. "You know this is too heavy for one person to carry."

He allows Amy to join in the struggle. They pull the creature further onto the shore. They pull and tug while dragging the heavy cadavers over pebbles and rocks far away from the beach and towards their home. The strain of pulling the body flushes both their pale cheeks, even so, Mat insists on moving the body totally clear of the incoming tides. One-minute turns into five. Five minutes turn into 15. And 15 minutes turn into an hour.

"Maybe we should try to resuscitate him," suggests Amy.

Mat agrees and reaches for the back of the body's head to remove the granite gray toned mask it appears to be wearing. It won't budge and he can't seem to locate where the mask ends, and the neckline begins. He wonders if this could really be an undiscovered mountainous creature the world has never seen before. He also wonders if this could be the real Bigfoot the community has labeled him to be. After studying the body even further, he makes a gruesome discovery. It's not wearing a mask or a costume. It doesn't appear to be human.

"Look at this," he gasps while motioning for Amy to take a closer look at the head of this creature. She hastily examines the body from head-to-toe and confirms her earlier suspicions about this being the find of the century. It is not human. She double-checks behind the ear lobes, under the chin and finally around the eyes to make a more thorough professional assessment.

"This is too much of a discovery for just us two. We need to let someone else know and we need to do it now," she tells him while backing away from the body.

"Did you see the same thing that I saw back there?" she wonders while the two of them hike back up the Aspen covered hill leading to their home.

"What exactly did you see?" he wearily asks.

"Something unlike anything I've ever seen in this world before," she replies. "It's scary! It's exciting!"

"I agree," he nods. "It's scary."

CHAPTER 8

DISAPPEARING ACT

Sheriff Winnow Pendleton arrives several hours after Mat first gave him a call. Mat directs the sheriff to the great room, his favorite room in the house.

"Is there too much sun in here for you?" Mat wonders after noticing Pendleton squinting a few times. The seven-foot windows lining the east wall usher in the glowing morning sunlight.

"Not at all," Sheriff Pendleton assures him without hiding his apprehension.

Pendleton's uneasiness is the result of hearing numerous tales about this recluse and his wife. He fears that even making eye contact will give way to the many outlandish stories he has heard throughout the years. And he suspects that the so-called "Big foot" will somehow detect that the sheriff is one of his greatest critics. Pendleton could've been there earlier, but instead, he chose to help the wife do laundry, feed the baby, and visit a few friends before answering the call. The dispatcher promptly tells him that the caller sounded desperate, even frightened, nevertheless, the call sounded suspicious to him since it came from Mat Crawford, aka big foot.

Amy stirs the pitcher of iced tea until the sugar completely dissolves. She is aware of how much her husband detests tiny granules of sugar to settle on the bottom of his glass. She carries the glasses of iced tea into the great room. The Sheriff sits up and gives an appreciative smile to her.

She sits on the wood serving tray on the coffee table that Mat made from a tree trunk.

"Thank you, Mrs. Crawford," Sheriff Pendleton politely responds, then, lifts the glass along with the napkin from the tray. He gulps it down before she has a chance to leave the room, but Mat still does his usual sip by sip ritual.

"Thanks Honey," Mat compliments and tells her.

"This is the best iced tea you've ever made." Amy nods and stares as he holds the glass up to the light and checks for sugar granules. Amy usually would've protested, but, for the sake of her guest, she decides to let it go.

"Would you like a refill?" she eagerly asks Pendleton.

"Oh no," he replies while sitting the empty glass down onto the coffee table. "One glass hit the spot. Thank you."

"So, you say this…" Pendleton pauses. "You say this creature drowned somehow and is now on the riverbank down the hill a way?"

Pendleton pays close attention to Mat's body language. When his head bobs yes, he makes a note of it. When Pendleton notices Mat's feet are firmly planted on the floor, he makes a note of it. Mat's eyes don't stray to the left or to the right as he meticulously describes the previous chain of events. He answers Pendleton in quick, concise words and without hesitation. Meaning, the Sheriff notes; he must be reliving factual events. Now, Pendleton is convinced that Mat and Amy did in-fact experience an unexplainable phenomenon. He believes this report has merit. However, he has concluded that the so-called creature is a man, not a Big-foot or anything else. He believes this creature is a man just like he is.

"Would you mind showing me where you left the body Sir?" he respectfully inquires.

Mat stands up to his feet. He is relieved that the Sheriff has taken them seriously.

"I'd be glad to show you," he replies in a voice filled with excitement. "Someone from the outside needs to witness this as well."

The nature of gravity moves them swiftly down the hill towards the lifeless body lying on the sand. When they arrive at the bank, to Mat's dismay, there is nobody there. He combs the bank for any possible signs or evidence and notices the imprint of the creature in the sand.

"See," he tells the Sheriff while patting the area where his mystery corps was last seen. "It's still warm." Pendleton pats the spot for himself and senses the warmth on his hand.

"You say it was dead?" he questions. "This body recently moved itself. "Look!" He shows Mat while pointing to deep foot impressions leading to the trail. "How heavy did you say this creature was?" he wonders.

Mat stoops down to study the footprints for himself.

"He or it was heavy," he pauses. "It's apparently, very heavy."

Without further explanation, Pendleton starts back up the hill and Mat follows close behind.

"What's the hurry?" Mat wonders. "Your wife!" Pendleton huffs as they climb up the hill. "We left her alone."

CHAPTER 9
THE EAGLE SEARCHES

Terry claws a 12-inch-deep hole into the ground and places her remaining catch-of-the-day in it. She covers it with dirt, then with leaves before searching the forest for a safe place to feast. Despite their differences, she wishes Cally were around to lead her to Frank. She consoles herself by holding on to the hope that he overcame the raging rapids and is someplace safe like she is. Now, her only desire is for them both to find each other. "I need rest," she tells herself. Her eagle-sharp eyes locate a cave high up on the rocky mountainside. The climb is steep, even so, she makes it and flings herself into the entrance of it.

"Is anybody in here?" Her quivering voice bounces from wall-to-wall throughout the empty cavern. She walks deeper into the darkness, allowing her eyes time to adjust.

"I'll only sleep for a little while," she assures herself while settling into a dry corner. Terry dozes off with Frank on her mind.

By the time Cally, Tom and G. W. realize their companions are gone, it is morning. Tom hopes the smell of the cooked meat will draw them back to camp. However, Cally senses that something has gone terribly wrong, and Frank and Terry need their help. So, they all set out to find them. Cally leads her companions through the wilderness where fallen leaves and twigs perform a dancing cadence underneath their feet. Cally plunges forward through the thickness of the forest by taking swift strides. She loops through narrow passageways then slows down for the sake of her wearied companions. They are so far behind; she fears they may get lost in the brush. G. W. decides to ride on Tom's shoulder instead of sticking with Cally. He figures cheering Tom on may be the best way to keep up with her. Suddenly, her descent down the steep hill slows to a crawl.

"What's going on?" Tom wonders and is surprised she allows him to catch up.

"I sense danger ahead," she answers.

The sound of rushing water catches her attention. Moments later, Tom loses his footing and begins to roll down the steep hill. He passes by Cally so fast that she couldn't stop his fall. G. W. jumps to the forest floor seconds later, Tom's fall is abruptly stopped by a tree.

"Are you okay? she asks while hoovering over him. Tom staggers to his feet. They all look on the other side of the tree and become very grateful. Beyond the tree is a deep gorge with a rushing river flowing through it.

"You're one lucky guy," G. W. tells Tom. "That tree was your fairy god mother. There is a 1 in 100,000 percent chance that you could have survived that fall. And had you survived there would've been a 100 percent chance of severe bodily damage.

"I know Frank and Terry came this way," Cally explains while pointing to skid marks recently made in the soil. They took a chance to get to the freshwater fish, so, we must take a chance to find them. Wait here," she insists. "I have to do this part alone."

Tom watches her disappear down the steep ravine and marvels at the sight of an enormous eagle mounting up into the sky. He doesn't realize that the eagle is Cally.

Mounting off the cliff, she spreads majestic wings, swoops down and around the suspected point of entry, then, soars along the shorelines in search of any signs of life.

CHAPTER 10

ALIEN IN THE ATTIC

The tall spruce tree extends its branches high above the 2-story over-sized log cabin. Its thick branches appear to reach for the attic window by scraping long narrow extensions against beveled glass. Frank hears the eerie sound in the distance and approaches the cabin with the utmost of caution. His instinct to survive overshadows all other needs. His water-logged body needs rest and plenty of it. So, he scrambles up the tree onto a thick limb. And then, Frank breathes a deep sigh-of-relief at the fact that it supports his weight. He pushes against the windowpane. It won't budge. He pushes again, only this time he pushes his shoulder against it. Still, it won't budge. He punches in a windowpane with one fist and causes the window to shatter into tiny pieces. Frank reaches inside, unlocks the metal latch, opens the window and squeezes through the opening into the attic.

While Mat shows the Sheriff their mysterious find on the shore, Amy cuts up the last of their home-grown potatoes and plops them into the pot of boiling water. The sound of the big spruce thrashing its branches against the attic window startles her. She hopes the sound of shattering glass was simply the wind kicking up the tree branches. Those hopes shatter at the unmistakable noise of footsteps overhead. Knots form in her stomach and Amy reaches for her inhaler.

"That tree is outdoing itself tonight," she nervously chuckles in between deep breaths from the inhaler. Amy quickly reassures herself that the sound must be a very big squirrel or a raccoon and goes back to her cooking.

The hike back up the hill from the beach put a strain on Mat's body. He looks back at the well-rounded sheriff whose face is also flushed.

"Don't worry about me," Pendleton's voice sounds strained and raspy. Mat is concerned about the sheriff since he is at least twenty years his senior. "Think about your wife. She's all alone." They continue to press up the hill.

Mat and Pendleton aren't conscious of the mud they track onto the freshly mopped kitchen floor. They simply barge into the house in search of Amy.

"Honey, where are you?" Mat calls while racing from room-to-room.

"Amy?" He calls and rushes up the stairs towards their bedroom in a panic. "Lord, let her be okay," he prays. The familiar squeak of their bathroom door draws him into the master bedroom suite. The sight of her standing at the bathroom sink washing her hands brings tears to his eyes. Those hands, he thinks, those delicate hands stringing that enormous harp is what drew me to her in the first place.

It was a recital put on by the music department of the school they both attended. Harvard University is their alma mater and the place where their love first blossomed. He had to make an appearance at the recital, not to play or even to listen, but to chaperone. She was so lovely, he recalls. He imagined her to be an angel fallen from the sky just to play for him, him alone. Her silky wavy brown hair, fair complexion, and sky-blue flowing gown mesmerized him at first sight. He was smitten with the love bug and could not shake his love for her, nor did he try. He was completely surprised to learn that she felt the same way about him. Her having love for him is still a mystery today.

"Is everything okay up there?" yells Pendleton while standing at the bottom of the stairs with one hand on his revolver.

Amy jumps when Mat enters the room.

"You startled me," she says. Mat just stands in the doorway. "Were you watching me wash my hands the whole time?" she curiously wants to know. "Why didn't you let me know you were back? You could've scared me to death."

Mat stands motionless and is unable to give a logical explanation without causing her undue fear and distress. He goes to the top of the stairs and salutes the sheriff.

"All is well up here," he winks, and the sheriff is relieved to be excused.

"Well?" the word lingers on her tongue as she walks seductively towards him. Her arms wrap around his strong neck, and she gently kisses him on the lips. "What do you have to say for yourself?" she smiles.

He gently grabs hold of her arms and pulls them down to her sides.

"The Sheriff awaits," he says while ushering her to the door with the wave of a hand.

"Dinner--?" her voice trails. "For two?" she winks.

"Just the two of us," he smiles.

"Where is the Sheriff?" she asks.

"I sent him home," he responds.

MAT COMPLIMENTS AMY WHILE pushing the dinner tray away. He helps by carrying an empty plate into their kitchen.

They huddle in the kitchen and playfully blow bubbles at each other. It's a ritual they practice on dinner nights, though, there is a lot more fun to come. Their eyes meet as if for the very first time. One caress from him leads to gentle kisses on the neck, cheeks, eyes, then, the lips. She falls into his loving embrace. The ritual becomes spontaneous, and the playfulness is a spawning ground for the act of true love. He notices her body is warm and trembling for his love as he slides his hungry mouth over hers and greedily satisfies his urge. To his dismay she loosens her grip and turns her head away from his.

"What's the matter?" he whispers while loosening his hold a bit.

"Did you hear that?" she questions and turns her eyes towards the ceiling. "I just heard something, and the sound came from the attic."

"I heard a sound earlier from the attic moments before you both returned," she recalls.

Mat steps back away from her. Distress and panic are written all over his face.

"So, why didn't you tell the Sheriff?" He earnestly wants to know.

She sighs, being disgusted with herself for not recalling the incident earlier.

"It slipped my mind," she explains apologetically.

Mat marches to the pantry, between the kitchen and the breezeway, in search of two flashlights. Then, he arms himself with a .45 magnum revolver, and heads for the stairs.

"Where are you going?" she questions while raising her voice to a squeal.

"To the attic," he emphatically replies.

"Not without me!" she insists and trails behind him up the stairs.

Frank hears the approaching humans on the creaking wooden stairs.

"Got to hide! Got to hide!" He panics and dumps a large box, contents and all, over his head.

The frigid mountain waters have seeped through layer after layer of feathers. He's wet right down to the bone and for the first time in his life his body won't stop shivering. Frank gives himself a bear hug to stop the shaking. Since his arrival on earth Frank has not experienced the elements until now. He wishes he would've stayed by the fire G. W. so gallantly provided. At least he would be warm and fed by now and under the constant watch of his greatest nemesis, Cally.

Mat enters the room carrying a heavy-duty flashlight in one hand and a revolver in the other. His eyes follow the illuminating glow as it penetrates the darkness in search of any signs of life. He glances back at the sound of footsteps and is relieved to see that it's Amy climbing the stairs.

A brusque wind whistles through the trees causing branches to brush against the attic window and outer wall.

"There's your sound," Mat tells her reassuringly.

"I suspected it was just that worrisome limb again," she chuckles while wishing it were true.

Mat cautiously leads the way and passes right by the big box to investigate the opened window. Amy stops to take a closer look at the box. She takes a double look at it before backing away and tripping over her own shoestrings.

"Whoa! Mat! The box!" she screeches.

He waives her towards the stairs and postures himself in front of the box. If I must confront this intruder, he thinks, I'll do it alone.

Amy, however, refuses to leave and picks up a nearby baseball bat. She played softball in college and was a powerful hitter, she recalls. If anything attacks us out of that box, she decides, I'll give him or it a good wallop with this bat.

With sweaty palms and trembling hands, Mat inches towards the jittery box.

"Come out of there!" he commands in a deeper-than- normal voice. "We know you're in there."

The box suddenly stops shaking and a squealing voice calls out, "You're not going to eliminate me, are you?"

Mat and Amy give each other a puzzled look while shrugging their shoulders. Frank lifts the box about an inch off the floor and peeps at the feet of his assailants.

"You'll be okay," Mat assures him and waves Amy back. "We only want to help you, that's all."

Mat's voice is beginning to have a calming effect on Frank. He senses a true sincerity in it and knows he can trust this human, at least for now. Then, Frank pushes up on the box revealing his clawed feet.

Amy shrinks back in fear and lifts the bat high above her head. Her heart races while she postures her body for a confrontation with the alien in her attic.

Frank props the box high enough to see Mat and Amy's face.

"Where should I put this box and its contents?" he politely asks in a matter-of-fact manner.

"Just put it anywhere on the floor," Mat sharply demands. He wants this intruder to know that he's no push-over.

Frank carefully places it on the floor where Mat indicates while giving them a look-at-me-I'm-harmless kind of grin.

The very idea of life existing beyond this planet has always been too far-fetched for Mat to even fathom. Here, he stands in a dusty old attic with the most exquisite specimen he has ever encountered. Amy looks on, baffled by the sight of it and the primate size of the cranium. During their studies at college, there never was enough proof to substantiate the existence of extraterrestrials. Even so, here stands a humanoid of unknown origin in their very own attic. The creature has the appearance of a man, yet the outward appearance is a dead give-away that it's not human.

"I suddenly have an epiphany!" Amy announces. "Could this be an experiment gone awry?"

Frank winches, then, snarls at her assumption.

"It's all right," she assures him. "We're not fans of exploratory surgery."

Frank grows weary of their curiosity. He's tired and hungry and can't wait a moment longer for a meal.

"Got anything to eat?" he blurts out.

Amy smiles and leads the way down the 2 flights of stairs to the kitchen.

"That sure was a long way down those stairs to this tantalizing food," Frank salivates and takes his liberty by opening cabinets to checkout their food inventory.

Mat and Amy's eyes meet and, suddenly, the room resonates with their laughter. They are amazed by how humanlike and intelligent this creature appears to be.

Amy warms up leftover soup in the microwave and prepares two meaty ham sandwiches for Frank. With that ferocious appetite, it takes two more servings of everything to satisfy him. He remembers his manners by thanking her with a lengthy roar and drawn-out burp.

"Oh!" gasps Amy. "You're welcome."

While Mat and Amy enjoy their coffee in the kitchen, Frank makes his way to the living room, turns on the TV, then, curls up on the sofa.

"What could he be?" Amy wonders after seeing him on the sofa. "He looks like an over-stuffed lizard, yet he appears to be domesticated."

"Listen," he says at the sound of the TV. "He's laughing at my favorite TV show. I don't know who or what he is, but I like him."

"Something happened," she says. "I wonder what led to him being washed down the river. Someone or something," she over emphasizes, is probably searching for him as we speak."

She pauses and the worried look on her face bothers Mat. "What do we do?" she asks.

Mat grabs her by the hand.

"We question him," he tells her. "And pray he'll tell us what we need to know before his people find him."

CHAPTER 11

TERRY'S HELP

In a dream, she feels herself falling, spinning, and spiraling down a black bottomless pit. Within this recurring dream, she waits, with great anticipation, to reach the bottom of the abyss, but every time, at the grand finale, she wakes up in a cold sweat. Terry's eyes pop wide open and not a moment too soon. The dawning of a new day slowly rises. She has the privilege of witnessing the splendor of light penetrate the darkness of the cave. A big black crow lands on a rock near the wide entrance. It calls repeatedly like it is trying to attract a mate. Terry eases her way towards the bird all the while thinking he'd make a delicious breakfast. The crow spots her and is not disturbed by her approach. He's used to park visitors throwing bread most mornings and suspects she will do the same.

"You mock me!" she yells while taking a flying leap towards the bird. "So, I will eat you!" she laughs, then, scoops the entire bird into her mouth.

Terry chides herself for sleeping too long while making her way down the side of the mountain to retrieve the next course. Sleeping through the night is highly unusual for a nocturnal creature like herself. Valuable time has been lost that could have been spent searching for her mate.

"I hope Frank found something as good to eat as this," she says while clawing her way into the damp soil. She buried her fish the night before and hopes to find it untouched by scavengers. "Yes! Yes! Yes!" her hands shoot into the air, as she shouts. "My fish are still here!" She devours her prey in moments. More food will be needed soon, but now she is driven by finding her mate rather than eating more food.

"Today is a new day and I will find my Frank," she declares while making her way back up the mountain to the cave.

One of her fondest memories of Frank comes to mind when she enters the cave again. She recalls using the Lizaradactiles mating ritual to first attract Frank's attention and decides to use it now. Terry knows if he is anywhere nearby, he'll come running. With both feet firmly planted on the ground and her knees slightly bent, she begins to howl. Her howl is startling and unfamiliar to the ears of the creatures in this forest. Birds quickly take flight; Deer dart to and fro; Rabbits hop back into their holes; and chipmunks huddle together in their nests. The thunderous cry travels above treetops and over mountain ranges. The cry quickly becomes the envy of wolves and the hope of coyotes. Even so, intuition tells her it has fallen upon deaf ears. While hunched upon a rock and with her head hung low, Terry is forced to conclude that Frank is nowhere to be found. She fears he is lost or even worse, dead.

Meanwhile, Cally hears the howl while trekking through the forest with Tom and G. W.

"Did you two hear that?" she wonders and halts the procession with the wave of a hand.

"What is it?" wonders Tom. The only sound he hears is the crackling of twigs and leaves beneath their feet.

"Yes, what is it?" echoes G. W. who heard the howls some time back but chose to dismiss it as a cry from a wild animal.

Her eyes widen as she turns to face the ridge above.

"It's Terry!" she exclaims. "That's the Lizaradactiles mating ritual cry I hear and it's not far off. If we hurry, we can be there by lunchtime."

Earlier, at the river she discovered a signature of their presence in the water. She hopes that both Lizaradactiles are up on the ridge, then, she'll no longer have to be the bearer of bad news.

They follow the trail leading to the top of the ridge. There, they find Terry standing near the entrance of a wide-mouthed cave still howling.

"Cally, is that you?" she shrieks. "I can't believe my eyes!" she tells her while jumping and leaping and circling around her. "Tom. You rascal, I can't believe you braved these treacherous woods just to find me," Terry blushes, then, gives him a heart-warming embrace.

"Where's Frank?" Cally wonders. "Is he with you?"

"No!" Terry answers and the jubilant visage turns into a flood of tears. "I don't know where he is," she cries. "We lost each other in the water. He fell in after I did and made it to shore on my own. I haven't been able to find him anywhere."

"I feel like he's alive somewhere," she confides, and tears roll down each cheek.

"He is indeed," confirms Cally who senses the same thing.

Terry tells of the events leading up to her and Frank's fall off the cliff. She tells of their plunge into the white-water rapids and the shock of being separated from him.

"The bond we have is real," she whimpers while resting her head on Tom's shoulder. "I just didn't realize it until that moment." Tom consoles her with a hug and gentle pat on the back. He looks to G. W. for help, but G. W. quickly avoids Tom's gaze with a wild cough. Tom turns to Cally in hopes that she'll somehow intercede, but only notices a raccoon in the place where she'd been standing.

Terry never realized how much of a bond she had with Frank until that moment. Their hearts had bonded long ago. When she'd vowed to remain his mate forever, she never imagined their bond would have to go through a test of endurance like this.

Terry yawns and stretches her arms towards the sky. She suggests they pursue Frank's trail after she takes a quick nap. "All of this talk about my ordeal has made me sleepy. I'm not used to this kind of stress," she whimpers then quickly disappears into the darkness of the cave.

Cally is ready to start searching for Frank right away. However, she's afraid of the opposition she'll surely encounter from her companions by making that suggestion now. While Tom empties his backpack and discovers there are only utensils and cooking gear inside, Cally comes up with a plan.

Cally goes down the mountain to the river and changes into a Lalooga, which is the fiercest sea monster known among her species. While in the river, she gulps up hundreds of fish, but decides to keep only 200. No need to be greedy and wasteful, she tells herself. Cally hopes her colleagues will be willing to listen to all she has to say when their stomachs are full of this fresh catch. Cally wants to leave before nightfall and believes Terry doesn't necessarily have to accompany them for Frank's rescue. She strings the fish together and carries all fifty of them up the mountain with ease.

"Hey guys, look at what I caught?" she boasts while giving the string of salmon and trout to Tom.

"I'm impressed," he admits.

G. W. helps by gathering enough wood and brush for building a fire.

"Here you are," he says while tossing a pile of wood at their feet. "I guess it wouldn't be polite to ask how you caught these fish so fast," G. W. snarls.

"You're catching on," she smiles.

"We all are," Tom adds.

While Terry sleeps, the smell of sizzling fish drifts into the cave. It makes its way up her nose and beckons Terry to follow it out into the camp. She obeys the urge and sleep-walks out to the cleaned fish lying on the ground. Tom and the others silently observe her methodically eat each fish. She starts by biting off the heads, then, works her way all the way down to the tail. She doesn't waste the tails either, she simply saves them for last. Within minutes the remaining uncooked fish are devoured, and she wakes up out of her slumber begging for more. Cally hadn't counted on Terry waking up at this time of day. According to Cally's calculations, Terry should be entering into a deep-sleep cycle by now. Without so much as a tap on the shoulder from anyone, here she is, just as Cally was about to suggest they all leave to search for Frank.

"Now that you're awake, want to go looking for Frank?" Cally hopes all will be as anxious to leave as she is.

Tom is fast asleep and using his backpack for a pillow.

"Look at him," says Terry. "I don't have the heart to wake him."

G. W. bends down to study Tom's face. "He's sleeping like a baby," he opens an eyelid, then, pinches Tom's cheek. "He's out like-a-light."

Cally grins. "Would you mind staying here to watch over him while Terry and I continue the search?" she begs.

"It seems like watching over him is all I've been doing lately!" he snipes while pretending to be bothered. "Okay," he agrees. "You two have fun."

Cally isn't quite sure about how to have fun under these circumstances and thinks about asking for clarification later.

G. W. relishes the idea of being Tom's protector and friend.

"I guess I will have my hands full protecting this human and the camp. You two go on without me." He commands with a sliver of a smile. "I'm needed here," he proudly proclaims.

CHAPTER 12

FRANK HANGS AROUND

A my wakes up early in the morning to Mat humming a tune in the bathroom. She looks at her bedside clock and notices it is half past 8. It is almost time for the sheriff to stop by and she needs to shower and dress before he arrives.

"He has to do better," she mumbles about Mat's slowness and hurries to the bathroom.

"Hurry up honey!" she shouts while barging in on him. "You don't have time to shave." She grabs the razor out of his hand.

"I'm hurrying. What's the rush?" he wonders.

"Well, you do need a shave," she admits after noticing his 5 o'clock shadow. "So, I'll shower while you groom," she tells him while getting into the shower.

She dresses and rushes downstairs fully expecting to see Frank snuggled on the sofa with the blanket and pillow she left him the night before. To her disappointment, the creature is not there. He left the blanket folded in a perfect square and neatly laid the pillow on top of it. Panic stricken, she tosses the pillow and blanket to the floor. Amy searches every nook and cranny of the room including under sofa cushions and the bear skin rug.

Frank is nowhere to be found. Amy hates having to admit it, but Mat was right when he suggested they tie up the alien.

She checks all the adjoining rooms. Then, after looking everywhere she can think of, Amy scolds herself for being too trusting. Amy races up the stairs to the bathroom where Mat is still showering. "Almost done honey," he detects her presence by the sudden chill in the shower.

"I surely hope so," she tells him in a winded shrill. "The sheriff is at the door as we speak."

"Okay," he calmly replies. "So, open the door, let him in." Mat wonders why she is so worried about him finishing up since she's already dressed.

"There is one major problem with that honey." Her voice quivers and she doesn't bother to conceal any apprehension.

"And the problem is," she tells him. Mat can tell if something is wrong.

"The alien is no longer on the sofa," she says. "He is no longer here."

MEANWHILE, THEIR VISITOR, SHERIFF Pendleton, is becoming increasingly agitated about the long wait at the door. The excessive knocking has penetrated the entire first floor and is rapidly ascending upwards towards their bathroom.

"You run downstairs and let him in. I'll be down in a few minutes," he explains. "Surely neither one of us wants him to disturb our new friend, wherever he may be."

"You're here early," she says while waving Sheriff Pendleton into the living room.

Mat and Amy agree that allowing their new discovery to be taken away would be a travesty. The alien is their discovery, so they reserve the right to be the first to communicate with it.

So, as soon as the Sheriff leans back on the sofa to assume a more comfortable position, she inconspicuously checks the area again for any evidence of their alien visitor.

"Your husband and I have a 9 a.m. appointment," he explains with his head cocked to one side. He looks puzzled by the overturned sofa cushions and various other items scattered around the room.

"Oh, really?" she pretends not to know about the meeting.

She's too nonchalant to suit his taste. His experience as a police officer tells him she is trying to conceal something. His suspicions rise more when she rearranges the floral display on the coffee table in front of him, for the third time. I'm sure Mat would have told his wife about their meeting, he reasons. It was no secret. I certainly would have confided in my wife about it.

"I guess it slipped his mind," he says while fishing for the truth in her soft hazel eyes.

"Would you like a cup of coffee and breakfast?" she politely offers. Her smile is warm and genuine this time. Mat always tells her she has a smile that could tame a beast. Amy hopes it will work for him.

"Well," he hesitates. "I'll take the coffee, but breakfast, well, that depends on what you're serving."

Amy browses through her pantry to see what she has on hand. "Good," she sighs at an unopened box of pancake mix. The all-too-familiar creak on the stairs is a sure sign that Mat is on his way down. She gives a sigh of relief. He strolls into the kitchen and grabs her from behind and kisses her on the cheek. "I'll take over as host from here," he tells her.

The batter is mixed, and the griddle is hot enough for the pancakes. She spoons them onto the hot surface, four at a time. If she hurries, she will have time to go to the pantry for two steaks, then, make it back in time to flip the pancakes.

"Ah!" she screams at the sight of their extraterrestrial visitor hanging upside-down on the rod they used to hang wet winter coats.

Amy cringes at the sight of Frank's large, clawed feet curled over the extended wooden rod. It is angled between the two back walls of the pantry. She rushes out of the room, slamming the door behind her. Mat and the Sheriff ran into the kitchen.

"I saw a mouse! There is a mouse!" Amy screams while pointing to the mudroom.

Pendleton cuts in front of Mat and reaches for the doorknob. "Please, don't open it," she yells.

Mat holds the door shut.

"I'm ready to eat and I'm sure you two are as well." She hopes Mat will catch on and follow her lead.

"Okay. Calm down," Mat says in a comforting tone. "We'll take care of the mouse after we eat."

Pendleton notices two mouth-watering steaks in Amy's hands and changes his mind about staying for breakfast.

"If steaks are what you're cooking for breakfast, count me in," he declares with a wide grin.

"Okay! You two get out of here so I can finish cooking," she orders while shooing them both to the doorway.

Mat turns to search her face for the truth about all that just happened. She acknowledges his gaze with a nod, then, tilts her head towards the mud room.

"We'll leave under one condition," Mat promises. "What's that?" she asks.

"No mice burnings," he jokes.

A roar of laughter erupts out of both men as they walk towards the living room.

Good, she thinks and uses this reprieve to peep into the mud room at Frank again. She can't help but wonder how long this creature will remain in this state. Judging from the time of day it is, she concludes, he must be a nocturnal creature. Also, she surmises that his layers of scales indicate he is a member of the reptile species. However, the feathers in the center of his back indicate he may be part bird as well.

In the living room, Pendleton jokes with Mat about the mouse and tells him that the mouse and the creature are one and the same.

"So where do you suppose this creature disappeared to?" Pendleton wants to know.

"I'm not sure," he answers hastily and arouses suspicion in the Sheriff.

Pendleton has known Mat ever since he moved up to their little mountain town. As a matter of fact, he was the only person protecting Mat's right to settle in the small community. He's not quite sure why Mat is holding out on him. Knowing Mat like he does, he is certain it must be for a good reason though.

Pendleton takes a long sip of hot black coffee.

"I may have to send for help with the search before the FBI arrives," he says.

"The FBI!" exclaims Mat. "You called the FBI?" he questions. The horizontal creases defining his forehead deepen.

"Well," Pendleton explains. "I called my superiors, and they called the FBI. Something like this is too big for you and me to handle on our own. We need to find out where this creature is from. Did he come from a lab or another world? Calling me to come down here is the best call you ever made. You could've saved the world!" Pendleton proclaims while making a shape of the world with his hands.

After breakfast, Pendleton is still hanging around. He knows if he pokes around enough the truth may come out whether they want it to or not.

"Gee, Amy that sure was a great breakfast. You're giving Gilda at the café a run for the money. I mean, their food isn't half as good as this."

"My pleasure," she tells him while gathering the dishes from his tray. He follows her into the kitchen where Mat is busy placing dirty dishes into the dishwasher.

"I measured the spot where this creature was lying. He or it must have been heavy. Those impressions in the sand are deep, very deep," Pendleton says while moving out of their way by leaning against the pantry door. "This creature may be dangerous, so, I've called a few of the locals to come here and comb through the surrounding woods," he tells them while repositioning towards the doorway. "It's time for me to go check on the posse," Pendleton yawns while stretching towards the ceiling. "Wow," he bows his head apologetically. "Good food makes me sleepy. Thank you, Amy, for the breakfast. It was great."

Mat and Amy watch him speed away in his Land Rover.

"Ooh, that was close," she nervously says, and then relaxes while watching her husband wash dishes. "Thanks for the help," she smiles and kisses Mat on the cheek. He blushes while bending over and placing another dish into the dishwasher. "Now, go take a look inside the mud room," she urges.

Mat gasps at the sight of Frank hanging from the rod.

"That's the same reaction I had," Amy giggles. "Only mine was accompanied by a scream."

He eases towards Frank and recalls Pendleton's last words on the matter. Is this creature really a threat to society, he wonders? Mat bravely moves closer to Frank until his nose is within inches of him. He carefully and cautiously examines Frank by poking and prodding while encircling him. This peaks Amy's curiosity to do the same, however, Mat motions for her to stay back with the wave of a hand.

"I believe it's nocturnal," she tells him. "He probably won't wakeup until sundown."

"Still," he says while meeting her at the pantry door. "I think we should leave him alone to rest."

They tiptoe back to the kitchen where she pours Mat his usual second cup of coffee, then, sits across from him at the kitchen table.

"No coffee?" he wonders after seeing her reach for the orange juice.

"No thanks. I think I'll have juice. I drank my second cup earlier." He stares into his mocha coffee with a troubled look on his face.

"I believe it's nocturnal," she lightheartedly announces. Her announcement doesn't break his stare into his cup. Whenever he stares into his cup this way, she knows something must be bothering him.

Suspicious eyes peered up at her. "So, he is a night predator," he concludes.

"I'm not certain he is a predator, yet. He's not human and he's not animal, so, I don't know what he's capable of," she confesses with apprehension.

Mat is not sure what he is capable of either. His only concern is for it not to harm them or anyone else for that matter.

"What do we do when it wakes up?" he worries.

Her warm slender hand slides over his.

"We feed it, then, we question it. If he gives us the right answers, we help him; the wrong ones, we turn him in."

He sighs, "Is it as simple as all that?"

"It's as simple as all that," she answers with her usual assurance. This assurance always causes Mat to be at ease, even amid turmoil, but not this time.

Mat moves his chair closer to hers. With one arm around her waist, he draws her warm body towards his. His hand gently moves up and down her spine, then, his hand massages its way up the spine to her neck. She is totally relaxed by his gentle touch. Her head gently falls forward in response to his touch, then, it moves to the side and towards wherever his touch leads.

"Honey?" he says while suddenly moving away from her.

Amy moans. She doesn't want this moment to end. "Yes dear." "Maybe we should turn him in now, while we have him contained." Deep down, she feels like defying common sense, just this once, and casting all her votes with this creature. She has a gut feeling that he is harmless and could really use their help right now.

"You saw him," she argues in defense of her stand. "He is so helpless. This is fate. You believe in fate, don't you? I believe fate wants us to help him get back to where he belongs."

Mat hopes she is right. He usually doesn't go by feelings or instinct, but for the time being, he feels led to give it a try.

CHAPTER 13
OUT OF THE BAG

Sheriff Pendleton pulls into Mat's narrow graveled driveway with FBI agent, Dan Schooner.

"I hate dropping in on them uninvited this way. He did ask me to come by tomorrow morning," explains Pendleton. "But last night Mat's voice sounded too shaky to be ignored. I told my wife, and she and I both agreed he sounded like he was nervous or frightened about something," Pendleton explains.

"So, your wife is in on this too?" Agent Dan wryly questions while giving him a look of disapproval.

"Oh, don't worry," the Pendleton assures. "She doesn't know about the creature. She only took the voice mail message for me."

Mat is tempted not to answer the door since he just snuggled down on the sofa for his afternoon nap. He can't imagine who could be calling, seeing how no one in town ever bothers to visit. The forcefulness of the knocking causes the stained-glass side panels to shake. Mat fears they may soon shatter if he doesn't respond soon. So, he forces his body to go to the door and yanks it wide open. The sight of Pendleton causes him to step back and eye the man by his side with suspicion.

"Mat," greets Pendleton.

"Sheriff?" Mat questions.

"Allow me to introduce Agent Dan of the FBI," he says in a throaty masculine voice.

"My pleasure, I'm sure," responds Agent Dan while pressing his way into the house.

Agent Dan believes it is his sworn duty to scrutinize Mat's every move. He doesn't dismiss the hesitation in Mat's voice. He notes Mat's reluctance to shake his extended hand as hostility. He concludes, this man in front of him is, without a doubt, hiding something. So, he has decided not to leave until he finds out exactly what it is.

Disappointing Amy is not on Mat's agenda today. Regardless, he tells himself, he must do the right thing for her sake. The right thing now is to turn the alien over to Pendleton and Agent Dan.

"Mat," called Pendleton. "Are you alright?" he worries.

Mat blinks. He didn't realize he was staring though he often reacts to stress this way.

"Excuse me," he apologizes while blinking excessively again.

"Now that you're here, have a seat. I didn't mean to be rude," he assures while escorting them into the living room. He motions for them to be seated on the sofa. Then, Mat settles down into his favorite brown leather chair near the fireplace.

"Well, we don't intend to take up too much of your time, but, that message you left for me sounded urgent. I rushed over right after I got it this morning," he explains. "After leaving place this morning I was contacted by the FBI. I faxed them a detailed report about our find on the beach last night. Agent Dan arrived at the airport about an hour ago," Pendleton explains all in one breath. "Are you holding anything at all back from me?"

"What's up?" Detective Dan studies Mat. He observes his body language first. He analyses Mat's facial expressions; and now, he waits to tear apart his every word. Mat has already decided to tell all and reveal the whole truth.

"Sometime after you left yesterday, Amy and I heard a noise in the attic. I wanted to investigate on my own, however, she insisted on joining me. I thought it would be a branch banging against a window, but when I got up there, that wasn't the case. We were about to leave when a large box in the middle of the room began to move on its own or so we thought. I asked the person to come out. He was more afraid of us than we were of him," he takes a deep breath and crosses one leg over the other. The Agent cuts an eye at the Sheriff.

"Where is this creature now?" Agent Dan wants to know. Now, there is no doubt that Mat is telling the absolute truth.

Mat points towards the kitchen.

"Show us," the Agent demands.

Mat believes he may regret this decision down the road. After all, this is the discovery of a lifetime. Amy will most assuredly be angry with him about it. Even so, he believes it's better to be safe now rather than sorry later. He submissively leads the way to the pantry. They walk cautiously through the kitchen. Mat holds his breath while opening the mud room door. The men gasp at the creature still hanging from his claws like a bat. He "Hmmm," Agent Dan responds.

"Interesting," comments Pendleton. "What's it doing?"

"He's nocturnal as far as we can tell," explains Mat.

With only 3 hours of daylight left, Agent Dan and Sheriff Pendleton call for back-up.

"Oh yes!" says Agent Dan to his support team. "Bring over a secure van to transport this thing in," he instructs while putting special emphasis on the word thing.

"You mean he's real?" asks the other agent over the phone.

Agent Dan lets him know in no uncertain terms, "Oh yes, very real."

An hour later, a black van pulls into the driveway.

CHAPTER 14

NO SMOKE AND MIRRORS

Frank's scent leads them to a two-story log cabin which is nestled on top of a hill just above the river's edge. Cally is certain he is inside. His distinct scent is in the air.

There is a small crowd of men and women dressed in black and gathered in front of the cabin.

"Looks like they're busy," notices Terry.

"Too busy for us to be staring at them in the open," Cally responds. Then, she motions for Terry, with the wave of a hand, to follow her towards a cluster of bushes alongside the dwelling.

In the meantime, a barrage of vehicles converges on the parking lot from every direction. Among the vehicles is a white van with the words, Big Sky News, stenciled on the sides.

"One picture of this "big foot" is all I need," Tammy Stanton, the Big Sky News reporter calculates. She's determined to become the next Big Sky News anchorwoman of Butte, Colorado.

One-by-one, people from the town and surrounding communities happen by Mat's place. Somehow, the news that something big is happening at Mat's place, was leaked to the entire community. Agent Dan blames Sheriff Pendleton and is pinning the blame on his wife.

Slow processions of looky-loos prompt the FBI to put up a roadblock. Some residents attempt to outsmart the authorities and bypass the roadblock by climbing the neighbor's trees to get a birds-eye view of these once-in-a-lifetime events.

Cally and Terry watch as men dressed in black file out of the back of a black van. The van backs up to the side door of the house and this is when they notice more men struggle while carrying a large steel net inside.

"Must be for Frank," she concludes.

"Oh! No!" Terry shrieks.

During the commotion, Cally sneaks into the unlocked back door. Terry follows close behind despite Cally's objections.

"If you are seen," she argues. "That will give them reason to fear an all-out invasion."

Even so, Terry ignores Cally's reasoning and is unwavering about finding her mate at any cost.

The back door empties into a narrow hallway lined with doors on both sides. The first door turns out to be a small closet. The second is a guest bedroom and the third is an office. The staircase is straight ahead and sandwiched between a crowded kitchen and a large dining area.

"What do we do?" Terry anxiously wants to know.

There appears to be no clear path leading to Frank. However, Cally has a plan that does not include Terry.

"Hide," Cally warns.

"What?" Terry squeals.

"You want Frank back?" Cally sharply asks.

"Yes, of course," she responds.

"Then, you must trust me on this and hide. Now!" She points to the closet they passed on their way into the house. Terry reluctantly makes room for herself in the tiny enclosure as Cally closes the door. Cally then inches her way towards the stairs where she decides to put her human sex appeal to good use.

"Hey, big fella," she seductively calls to the man standing near the bottom of the stairs.

"Do we know each other?" he wonders while strolling down the narrow hallway to greet her.

"Where have you been hiding?" he wonders with a sensuous smile.

"Oh, I've been asleep in the guest bedroom," she slyly replies and slides out of her jacket to reveal a slender hourglass figure.

"Would you care to join me?" she entices while wetting smooth voluptuous lips. Cally arches an eyebrow and lifts a taunt chin to signal him to follow her.

"Why aren't you wearing a uniform like the other men?" she wonders. As they pass through the doorway of the guest bedroom, she draws his body close to hers by pulling his narrow black tie. He falls to the bed directly on top of her.

"I love a man in a suit," she whispers.

Her tongue gently brushes against his cheek. She teases his lips with a wet tongue. He doesn't know she is tapping into his thoughts and persuading him to want her. Cally's amazed at how easily he falls under the spell of lust. She senses his loneliness and desperate need to be loved.

"Close your eyes Agent Saunders," she tells him, then, proceeds to peel off his clothes, one item at a time. He helps her with each item and even kicks off his shoes, all the while, thinking that she's doing the same.

He wonders how she knows his name. It's a fleeting thought that leaves as quickly as it comes.

Now that she has won his trust, she climbs on top of him and runs her fingers alongside his temples. Smooth slender fingers run down his neck. Her hands find his pressure points and quickly render him unconscious. Cally leaves him sleeping peacefully and transforms into his likeness.

She senses Frank is in the vicinity even though he is hidden from view. With ease, Cally worms her way through a small crowd huddled around the back door of the kitchen. Her nose leads her into the mud room where Frank is assuming a harmless, yet awkward position. She thinks he looks like meat hanging from a butcher's meat hook. Surrounding him is a man holding a gun; two others are securing a net beneath Frank's drooping head; and a fourth man is attempting to pry his clawed feet loose from the hook. Cally has shapeshifted into Agent Sanders whose seniority becomes clear the moment she enters the room.

"Sir, what do you suggest we do now?" the fourth man asks Agent Sanders who evidently has authority over them.

"This creature's claws are clamped tight around this hook. I can't get them to budge," he complains.

"Well," she pauses. "Everybody needs to clear out of here and give me room to think!" she orders while pushing them towards the door. "And take this silly net with you," she orders while tossing the net at the door and clipping the last man in the butt.

The only thing that will wake Frank up, at this stage of his rest, is the scent of food. She rummages through the cabinets and refrigerator for food and finds nothing he would like. Then, she checks the freezer and hits the jackpot: thick T-bone steaks. Fortunately for her, Agent Sanders has a lighter in his pocket. She knows this is just the thing needed for heating the steak.

Fat dripping from the steaks is beginning to drizzle down onto Frank's chin and gradually into his mouth. Frank releases his grip, flips, then somehow, lands on his feet. The steak is devoured within seconds and leaves him groaning for more.

"More," he belches while licking his fingers.

Cally pushes him towards the door. "It's me you fool!" she tells him.

"You have more important things to worry about," she scolds while in the body of a man.

He never thought he'd be happy to see Cally again and promises himself to tell her someday, but not while she looks like a man.

Outside, Pendleton attempts to disperse the crowd with the help of Brumby, his deputy.

"So much for not attracting attention," he tells him.

"All right now, everyone listen-up!" he yells into the crowd. "This is not a circus. It's a private affair taking place at a private residence," he continues while waving the crowd to move back. Despite his pushing and prodding, the crowd only moves back a measurable inch. This angers him so much that he pulls out his revolver and shoots it three times into the air. FBI agents dive for cover behind whatever and whoever is closest to them. The rest of the crowd scrambles underneath nearby vehicles, trees, and bushes and some even hold up their hands in surrender.

Brumby is baffled by the gunfire and backs away from Pendleton in protest. He suddenly recalls that Sheriff Pendleton is known and feared amongst the townspeople for doing the unexpected when you least expect it. However, this is a side of him his deputy has never witnessed before.

"When I say clear out, I mean clear out!" Pendleton yells while resting both hands securely on his hipster gun holster and standing straddle-legged on the front lawn. "Pack your stuff and get off this property!" he demands.

The startled crowd disperses in every direction, no questions asked.

Meanwhile, like a leopard patiently waiting for its midnight meal, Cally lies in wait. Her expression softens at the sound of Pendleton's announcement. She has been hoping for the crowd around the house to thin out. Now, she and her comrades will be able to slip out into the night, undetected.

During the melee, feet scamper on the other side of the mud room wall and she senses the house being emptied. Screeching tires and ricocheting rocks rattle the screen door. She is assured that the opportunity to free Frank has finally arrived. Cally calculates the next move and casually strolls into the kitchen under the disguise of the FBI agent she's impersonating. Along the way, she picks up a coat and a knit skull cap and hopes it will be large enough to conceal Frank's head.

"Put this on," she orders while holding the coat up for him to slip both arms into its sleeves. He shrugs at the tight fit around his shoulders. She hands him the hat and with ease he stretches it over his head, but it fails to hide his disfigured skull.

"That will have to do," she tells him while taking his arm and coaxing him to the door. The unsuspecting officer keeping watch at the door allows them to pass without question. She didn't expect it to be so easy and from this incident begins to discover that there is a bond between some humans that will later prove impossible to break.

"This creature may sleep until the sun goes down," she tells the agent at the door of the closet. "No need in us all starving, right? Why don't you take about 10 of those steaks into the kitchen and put them on that stovetop grill for anyone who wants one. I'll watch your post," she assures him.

The officer attempts to enter the house through the mudroom until she blocks his way.

"I'm trying not to disturb him, so, I took the steaks into the kitchen already, so go around front. They'll be on the counter."

As Frank steps outside, the chill of the brisk mountain air stings his face. The brightness of the moon reminds him of the sun. Now he's hungrier than ever. His stomach is beginning to growl and churn and make him feel uncomfortable.

"Go, hide behind those trees while I get Terry out of there," Cally orders.

News of Terry being in the house is a total surprise to him. His mouth drops wide open. Stunned by the news, he grabs her by the arm.

"Did you just say that Terry, my wife, is in that house?" he questions. He can hardly believe his ears and wonders whether he heard Cally correctly. When he saw Terry plummet off that cliff, he lost sight of her in the raging river. Frank thought she'd died, and his world had ended right then and there.

"Terry is in the house!" He raves and practically does a somersault on the lawn. "How did this happen? Who brought her here?"

He loses sight of reason and bolts towards the house. Luckily, Cally tackles him, and he tumbles to the ground before an approaching officer notices.

"Are you crazy?" she yells through clinched teeth. "Let me handle this, then, we'll all make it out alive."

Frank had to admit that her suggestion makes more sense than him stomping his way into the cabin. After all, he reasons, Cally did successfully rescue him and she's been brooding over them all, like a mother hen, ever since they arrived on planet earth.

Cally enters the cabin a second time and goes virtually unnoticed. Terry is no longer in the closet underneath the stairs, so Cally must rummage through every conceivable hiding place she can think of to locate her. Her unassuming disguise makes it easy to check every nook and cranny of the two-story home to no avail. She puts her senses to work for her; however, these abilities always diminish when assuming another form. With this being the case, she reverts to her original human form to enhance her senses. Her nose leads to the last unchecked second closet located beneath the steep staircase. "Bingo!" she says aloud. Terry is dangling by her clawed feet upside-down from a wooden coat rod.

Cally empathizes with Terry. The stress of this unusual situation is enough to bring anyone down.

"Don't worry my friend," Cally thinks aloud while sizing-up the situation. "I'll get you and Frank back together somehow."

She pokes and prods to pry Terry's feet from the rod. They won't budge. Terry appears to be a permanent fixture in the closet. As a matter of fact, her clawed feet tightened their grip around the rod when she touched them. Cally comes up with a fail-safe plan. One whiff of this gum is all it will take to wake her, Cally reasons. Food is a mainstay for these creatures, she recalls, so this will do the trick. Unless a Lizaradactile senses imminent danger or catches a whiff of food, any kind of food, they will not wake out of a sound sleep. Like smelling salts, Cally slowly waves the fresh cinnamon gum before each nostril until Terry takes a whiff.

"Come on dear," she coaxes. "Take a long deep breath," she begs while holding the gum under her nostrils. Terry gracefully flips to the floor and without uttering a word, removes the gum from Cally's hand and gobbles it down, wrapper and all.

"More!" she demands.

Cally snatches a jacket hanging on a hanger and drapes it over Terry's shoulders. Terry gives her a nod of gratitude, and then, follows Cally out of the closet.

"Frank is hiding behind the two tallest trees out back," Cally whispers. "Go join him and wait for me there."

After shedding Agent Sanders' suit and changing back into her girly form, she gives him a surreal fantasy of reliving his childhood desire to become a clown. Moments after she exits the room, he wakes up shivering uncontrollably and wearing nothing but his underwear.

He finds his suit neatly folded at the foot of his bed. He jumps to his feet the moment he remembers there is an alien in the house.

"The alien!" he shouts while jumping out of bed and dressing faster than he has ever dressed in his life. Agent Sanders is totally puzzled by the feelings of achieving his childhood dream of becoming a clown. He wonders who wouldn't desire to become someone who promotes cheer, and then, smiles at the thought.

Outside, Cally urges Frank and Terry to hurry. "They'll be on to us soon.

Cally leads the way back to the place where they left Tom and G. W. The grueling hike is treacherous for Frank and Terry. She leads them down the steep hill to the river's edge. From there, they scurry along the narrow-jagged edge of the riverbank towards their destination.

Back at the house, Agent Sanders enters the kitchen from the direction of the mudroom. He is too caught up in his thoughts to notice the stares coming from the other officers in the room.

"Smells good," he says while sniffing the aroma of grilled steak.

The cook, who is Officer Murphy, beams with pride. Agent Sanders looks on and wonders why this officer, whom he assigned to guard the alien 24/7, is cooking steaks. He enters the mudroom to check on the alien and makes a startling discovery. The Alien is not there. The net he ordered is on the floor and the officers assigned to stand watch outside the door are all in the kitchen.

"What happened? Where is he?" Agent Sanders shouts. He circles the area where the alien is supposed to be. "He was the find of the century!" he weeps while falling to his knees. "Who moved him? Who? Without me knowing about it?"

He summons the other officers and demands an explanation. Officer Murphy is totally confused and offers no explanation or reason for leaving his post. He is immediately put on administrative leave and is ordered, by Agent Sanders, to exit the premises. The other officers filed out behind him.

"Wait a minute," Agent Sanders calls to them leaving with Murphy. "Where is everybody going?"

"If Murphy leaves, we all leave," answers rookie Officer Clare.

"What the hell for?" wonders Sanders.

"We all were in the kitchen enjoying steaks because of you. You told Murphy to cook the steaks while you watched the—the—Alien," he stutters. "So, now you're putting the blame on him for everything, that sucks."

"Yeah, that sucks," agrees another officer.

"Officer Murphy, who gave you permission to leave your post?" questions Sanders.

"Well," he hesitates while glancing back at his fellow officers. "Well, you did, sir. And you promised to take my place while I cooked the steaks."

"What!" Sanders shouts, then, he pauses when the image of a beautiful woman enters his thoughts. "That's ridiculous. I never said anything like that to you. And where did these steaks come from anyway?" He hopes to solve this mystery without letting anyone go. Too much paperwork, he tells himself. Glimpses of himself and this mysterious woman in a compromising position enter his mind again. He wonders where memories of this woman are coming from. Above all, he wonders where reality ends and this fantasy begins.

"Why, you Sir. These steaks came from you," answers Officer Murphy without hesitation.

Agent Sanders shakes his head from side-to-side and reveals his frustration with a low grunt.

"No one has answered my first question yet!" he shouts. "Where is the Alien? If you don't know, then, we all need to split up in twos and search the Rockies for it right now. Get moving!" he demands while slamming his fists down on the granite countertop.

No one is as confused by this line of questioning as Murphy. He thought for sure that Agent Sanders spent the last forty minutes alone with the intruder. If he spent the last forty minutes alone with this creature, he reasons, there is no way that he can blame anyone other than himself for its disappearance. Murphy hopes this matter won't end with the need for a court hearing. He feels like reporting Sander's suspicious behavior is his only recourse.

Murphy calls the Director of their FBI unit and tells the details of the incident.

"I'm telling you Sir; this creature has altered his memory somehow. He doesn't recall ordering us to put the net down or to leave the room or anything," Agent Dan, FBI District Director, has his eyes fixed on a lone spot on the wall of the surveillance van while Murphy unloads on him.

"He doesn't recall placing the stack of steaks on the kitchen counter for his officers to grill," Murphy anxiously informs him. "And now he's in there chewing our heads off about the escape of the alien he was supposed to be guarding."

Agent Dan grimaces at the news and rakes oversized burley hands through short cropped blond hair. Dark roots paint his scalp and cause the platinum blond crew-cut to look even blonder. His ruddy complexion turns red in the heat of rage he displays at the news of the escaped intruder.

"What the hell! The alien has escaped. Why didn't you mention that in the first place?" he shouts while shooting to his feet and heading for the exit. He forgets to duck though, hits his head against the door frame, misses his first step and stumbles out of the van.

He orders his agents to detain Agent Sanders for questioning and to search the house for any signs of Frank. Meanwhile, he prepares himself for the snide remarks bound to come his way from the smug Sheriff Pendleton.

PENDLETON FINDS OUT ABOUT the FBI losing the alien. Shortly after Agent Dan gets the news, he decides to pay Pendleton a visit.

"Ah!" Agent Dan shutters at the sneer of the voice behind him. As he suspected, it is none other than his greatest nemesis, Sheriff Pendleton.

"Leave it up to the big boys is what I was told," Pendleton smirks. "Now look at what happened. He escapes. The find of a lifetime slips right through your little FBI fingers."

His words penetrate deep into Agent Dan's heart and his blatant laughter is like piercing jabs vibrating throughout his very being.

Dan responds with rapid fire commands.

"We need to send a team out to search the area. My boys aren't familiar with this rough terrain. That's where your boys come in. We'll need your help with tracking and maneuvering around these steep mountains."

Sheriff Pendleton sticks his chest out while proudly wearing a shrewd grin. "No problem-o," he responds, then, whistles for Deputy Brumby to prepare for the search. "We'll start at the first sign of light. I'll order a chopper too."

CHAPTER 15

SHUT IN

Outside of the cave, G. W. helps Tom make a security system using rope and a few empty cans.

"I hope this works," Tom says.

"Stop worrying. Everything I create works," boast G. W.

The night is cold, so Tom sits close to the campfire and rubs his hands together.

"You look exhausted," notices G. W. "Why don't you get some sleep while I keep the first watch.

Tom doesn't bother to argue with his little friend. He can hardly keep his eyes open. He grabs the blanket out of his backpack, curls up in a ball near the fire, and falls asleep. Moments later G. W. hears someone approaching the camp. Whoever it is, stumbles over the first line of defense, the rope. Then, they wrangle the cans and fall into the bushes.

"It's me!" the intruder announces. "Frank."

G. W. races to Frank and unties the string of cans wrapped around his ankles.

"These woods are no longer safe," Cally warns. "We need to leave as soon as we can pack up our gear."

"And Frank," she adds while extending a helping hand to lift him to his feet. "You should be more careful. Stop fighting with those cans and string," she jokes. They roar into laughter and relief that Cally has humorous side.

They pack up their gear and journey into the forest before sunrise. Traveling at night is not a problem for the aliens, but Tom struggles to see in the dark. He stumbles along the way more than he'd like to and is assisted once, twice, even more times than he cares to count, by his littlest visitor.

At dawn they finally make it back to their camp and are all anxious to get back to the city. The wilderness is Frank and Terry's domain. Even so, they have come to terms with the mistake they've made by wandering away from the camp. The thought of being cooped up in Tom's tiny apartment never sounded more appealing than now. Nearly drowning by falling into the Colorado Rapids and being held captive by humans is more than they ever expected would happen.

The ride home is deafly quiet. Everyone is exhausted, and luckily for Tom, even the Lizaradactiles ride in silence. Terry nestles in her seat next to Frank while resting her head on his shoulder. Frank doesn't protest like he normally would, and he has a tight grip on her hand.

Finally, in the early hours of the morning, they pull into the parking lot of Tom's apartment complex.

"Quiet you guys," he says in a hushed tone. They file into his apartment one-by-one while carrying the gear. Frank and Terry immediately perch in the hall closet, upside-down. And Cally grabs a blanket and curls up like a cat, on the sofa. Then, Tom retreats to his room, allowing G. W. to tag along and sleep wherever he chooses.

The next morning, Tom decides to prepare new ground rules for his visitors. He doesn't want to take their freedom away, no not by any means. However, he knows he must do everything he can to prevent compromising the mission.

So, Tom comes up with a speech and gathers the visitors into the living room for the meeting.

"Anything wrong?" she wonders while feeling his grief.

"Yeah, is anything wrong?" Frank parrots while stretching and walking towards them.

"From now on," he pauses and debates whether to tell them his dilemma or not. He is supposed to make their stay on earth as pleasant as possible, nevertheless, the only thing he can think to do is confine them to their rooms. Of course, they don't have their own rooms, so, they will be confined to the apartment.

"Frank," he says. "You and Terry must promise to remain in my apartment at all times," he tells him. "Don't answer the phone. Don't answer the door. Don't go outside for any reason." He looks to Cally for support, and she nods in agreement. "And Frank," Tom reminds him with a worried look on his face. "I'm sure the government took plenty of pictures of you while you were asleep. They will search for you in every place possible, so don't go outside uncovered."

CHAPTER 16

BACK TO WORK

"The boss is finally in the house," Tom mutters as Shakeam whizzes by. "I wonder why he's in such a hurry today."

Shakeam signals Tom to follow him and then quickly closes the door behind him. Tom believes he's being invited into the office to help with a special project. To his surprise, work is the farthest thing from Shakeam's mind.

He's anxious to forge ahead at developing a relationship with Cally. Shakeam, being a lady's man, has promised himself never to allow a woman to capture his heart again. His last relationship left his heart in ruins. He perceives that Cally is intelligent, beautiful and everything in between. She strikes him as naïve, in a good way, and he believes Tom can help him win her over.

"How was your vacation?" Shakeam wants to know.

"Coffee?" Tom offers.

Being fed-up with lying, Tom concludes the less said about his personal life the better. He wonders how to downplay their six-day excursion without becoming too obvious. Should I tell him the truth about our vacation, which turned into four days of mayhem and an unwanted workout? Tom remains level-headed about the situation. He'll simply tell him about the food; how long it took to prepare it; and that it was tender, juicy, and savory. Then, he reasons, if he wants to know more, he'll give a detailed account of the beauty of the mountains.

There's a faint knock at the door causing Tom to turn around.

"It's open," Shakeam commands.

To their surprise, it's Laura. Tom can hardly conceal his excitement the moment he lays eyes on her. He tells himself that Shakeam must wait.

CHAPTER 17

RESTLESS DESIRES

A week has passed since their trip to the mountains and the term "stir crazy" is being acted out by the visitors in Tom's one bedroom apartment. Frank and Terry bicker to the point of physically throwing blows at each other every chance they get. Cally pulls them apart whenever she's in the room, but most times she retreats to the bathroom during their waking hours. Neighbors complain whenever the ruckus begins, however, Tom sleeps through it all, leaving Cally to handle it.

Cally is fidgety as well, though not from staying inside. She has a strong desire to be with another human and this human is Shakeam. She doesn't understand these emotions and feels uneasy about them. Nevertheless, for the sake of research, Cally has decided to indulge Shakeam by secretly talking with him on the phone. For the past five days, she has convinced herself that their lengthy conversations are nothing more than research. Even so, something she did not anticipate was happening to her. Her emotions are running wild with desire. She would like to see him every waking moment. Her palms sweat at the very thought of him. She feels possessive and territorial about him like a beast over its prey. Her heart is claiming Shakeam as her own and hers alone. Logic persuades her to back away and logic has never failed her before. It has never lost a battle, but this time, her logic is losing ground. It is slipping away without her permission and Cally is afraid of the feelings that have overtaken her will. Cally wonders if this could be the human emotion known as love. She wants to know him intimately. Her heart throbs at the thought of Shakeam.

Unable to resist the urge to see him any longer, she finally accepts an invitation to join him for dinner and a movie. She knows that Tom will vehemently disapprove of her ever-seeing Shakeam on her own. Nevertheless, she will assure him that the date will be solely in the interest of research.

"That's it," she proudly and confidently reassures herself. "In the interest of research."

Later that night, the steady hum of worn kitchen appliances and Frank rummaging through his few belongings in search of a hooded robe, are the only sounds in Tom's apartment.

Terry stands guard at the closet door occasionally raising, then, lowering a hand his way to let him know no one is coming.

"You'll wake everybody up," she whispers after telling him to stop tossing Tom's shoes to the floor.

His robe is nowhere to be found, so Terry suggests they put their excursion off for another night.

"Where could it be?" he moans while stepping backwards out of the small walk-in hall closet.

"We'll simply have to ask Tom about it in the morning," Terry sighs. She fears he will suspect the less than pure, intensions. And the delay gives Terry second thoughts about venturing out without Tom's permission.

The following morning, though, Tom leads them right to their hooded capes. They were on the floor in a pile of the unwashed clothing worn on the camping trip.

"Sorry guys," he humbly apologizes as he absentmindedly scratches his scalp. His yawn assures them he's still tired and certainly not suspicious at all about their inquiry.

"I haven't had a chance to go to the Laundromat yet. Tomorrow is Saturday and my day off," he tells them while blinking. "I'll go first thing in the morning," he assures them. "Another sleepless night," he thinks aloud, while heading towards the door.

"These clothes are kind of smelly," complains Terry while clamping her nose with two forefingers. She scatters the soiled garments all over the floor until she spots their robes. "Finally," she grins. "I can tolerate our own smelliness, but no one else's," she confesses. "Whoa!" she says while catching a whiff of his robe and tossing it to him. "This one is the smelliest of all," she chuckles.

"Hey!" protest Frank. "That's my robe you're tossing around!"

"Sorry," she sheepishly apologizes.

Frank holds the robe at arm's length after sniffing it for himself.

"Whoa!" he declares. "It does smell disgusting. Something drops out of the pocket and falls to the floor. "Um…What's this?" he wonders while lifting the card to the early morning light shining through the living room window.

Terry breathes down his neck and strains to peer over his shoulder at the card. He flips it over only to discover writing on the back.

"Halo—ween," he says in a crude attempt to sound out the first word phonetically.

"Ooh, I know, I know!" Terry shouts with both hands waving through the air. "I know--I know!" she repeats enthusiastically, and one hand reaches for the air like grade-school children requesting permission to speak.

"Would you mind sharing this juicy bit of information with your mate?" he says, then quickly claps both hands over his ears to protect them from her squeaky shrill.

"No problem-- No problem!" she tells him.

Suddenly, she realizes she is mimicking the voices of nuns she heard on TV last night. She didn't realize the movie she watched would have this type of an impact on her. The movie To Sir, With Love, reminded her of the past when she fell madly in love with her trigonometry teacher in 2nd grade. Only her love interest had two arms, three legs, and magnificently flawless, green marbled skin.

"Halloween Party!" she reads without hesitation. "This is from the man at the theater," she recalls while triumphantly clapping her hands together.

At first, Frank is both annoyed and puzzled since he doesn't recall ever meeting this stranger.

"You wouldn't remember him," Terry tells him. "You were eating popcorn at the time. There was a man there in a booth who told us about a strange custom called Halloween and that our costumes were the best he'd ever seen," she explains. "He said there will be food and plenty to drink too."

Frank perks up in an instant. "When is this Hallo—een?" he demands.

"I'm not sure, but I bet G. W. can tell us. We must keep this secret from Cally," she insists. "There is no doubt, we can trust G. W. if we agree to take him with us. But that Cally will object," she snarls at the mentioning of her name.

"Hey G. W.," whispers Terry. "We have a favor to ask you."

He agrees to search his databases for information on the custom humans call Halloween.

"Aah… here it is, also known as All Saints Day. A mid-evil custom, controversial among some Christian sects, but we should be safe at a Costume Party, so to speak. Oh, here it is, held on October 31st of each year. Also known as Beggars Night, and Druids or witches would collect their sacrifices or people to sacrifice on this night. Now-a-days, it's a fun, festive time for feasting and celebrating the official end of harvest," he concludes and finally pauses to give them a chance to digest it all. "Where is this celebration to be held? Will it be nearby?" he wonders now that they've stirred his curiosity.

Frank and Terry's wondering eyes meet.

"We hoped you could tell us." She confesses.

He searches his databases for that specific information. "No!" he says emphatically. "I have no record of a central location for Halloween celebrations. Do you know the person giving the party?" he asks.

Terry snatches the card from Frank's hand and gives it to G. W. He scans the information that appears to be the size of a large poster board in his tiny hands.

"Looks to me like one of you should call this number for a location and time and don't wait too long seeing how Halloween is only 3 days away."

CHAPTER 18

DINNER WITH THE BOSS

The Nebula where Cally is from seems so far away and somehow unimportant on this special evening. Nothing will dampen Cally's spirits on this night, and she lets Tom know she's not even bothered by the fact that G. W. will be accompanying them. Tom has agreed to their date under one condition, that is if G. W. is their chaperon. She tried to convince him that their seeing each other again was in the best interest of scientific research. However, he wouldn't buy it. She knows deep within herself that science has nothing to do with it, unless, of course, love could possibly fall into this category. She feels like a woman for the first time in her shapeshifting life and doesn't care to change or shapeshift into anything else ever again.

Later that evening, Shakeam takes Cally to a restaurant, fully equipped with a jazz ensemble playing sensuous soft tunes that sweetens the mood. Soft candlelight creates an aura around everything in sight, including her love interest, Shakeam. Cally suspects he has something special to share with her simply by reading the silence during their meal. She is tempted to enter his thoughts while the waiter serves them lobster Newburg and stuffed crab. As the Caesar salad is hand tossed in front of them, she contemplates pulling whatever he is keeping from her out of his mind.

Then, she concludes, that would be an invasion of privacy. She has decided to always respect and honor this human.

"So, what's on your mind?" she finally musters up enough courage to ask.

He dips a small piece of lobster into the hot buttery sauce and slowly lifts it to his mouth. A small amount of sauce drips down over his chin causing Cally to instinctively reach over with her napkin and gently wipe it away.

"Would you mind terribly if we skipped the movie bit tonight, and instead, go someplace where we can talk?" he asks while summoning a passing waiter for the bill. Cally senses his uneasiness while noticing that he left his delectable dessert untouched.

"Are you going to eat your dessert," she asks while reaching across the table for it.

Her candor brightens his face with a smile. He wants to believe that she cares for him as much as he cares for her. Some of the anxiety subsides at the thought and he finally concludes, he will ask her to marry him tonight?

"Well, do you mind?" he asks again and smiles at the way she has buried her face in the chocolate mousse. She scrapes the dessert goblet for the last remaining morsel and leaves traces of it around the corners of her mouth, nose, and chin.

"Why should I mind so long as we're together," she tells him just when he reaches over with his napkin to wipe the chocolate away.

"I suspect your cousin wouldn't approve, but…" he adds, "I was hoping we could go to my place to talk in private."

Cally has already been warned by Tom about these kinds of propositions. She has done her best to assure him she will never be naïve enough to fall into that kind of trap. Somehow, even without using her sensory perception powers, she feels like Shakeam's motives are pure. She accepts his proposition and decides to leave G. W. in the car rather than to risk him interfering with and spoiling her perfect night out with the one human she truly cares about.

THE RIDE TO SHAKEAM'S apartment is virtually silent. Along the way, Shakeam takes her hand into his. Her very being appears to melt and bow down to his will. G. W. is suspicious of their silence and after the car stops, he becomes panicked the moment he hears the car doors open, then, close again. He suddenly realizes Cally purposely left him in the car inside her designer bag. He is certain that Cally would not absentmindedly leave her Gucci bag in the car.

"She's up to something and I will find out exactly what it is. "I'll find you!" he swears.

G. W. manages to pull the knife, he always carries, out of his pocket and rips through the leather seams of her bag. He steps out onto the leather covered seat and gives the area a wild-eyed inspection for a way out. Just then, he manages to locate the door locks and the door flings open while he still has a firm grip on the handle. He finds himself dangling over wet pavement, so he jumps down and slams the door behind him. The light of the full moon points to a clear pathway to the stairs leading to an apartment building.

"Ah, fresh air, there's nothing like it," he beams until a jogger and his black dog happen by. The short-haired Labrador leans towards him, barks, growls, then, takes a quick whiff.

"Come on, Bruno! Leave that doll alone," says the young man holding his leash. The dog whines a bit before obeying his best friend and trots away wagging a long wiry tail.

CHAPTER 19

FORBIDDEN PROPOSAL

S he knows Tom believes it is wrong for her to desire this human… this man. Despite this reasoning, she doesn't have the willpower to walk away.

Shakeam dims the lights as he ushers her to the leather 2-piece Sectional.

"Have a seat and make yourself at home. I'll be back in a moment," he assures then disappears into another room. Shortly afterwards, a soft ballad, pleasing to Cally's ears, begins to resonate throughout the apartment. In his absence, she admires the décor and finds the tan leather furnishings both seductive as well as inviting.

A corner light flickers and mimics flames of fire by casting shadows throughout the room and the ambience it creates adds to her vulnerability and weakness of heart. Cally's emotions betray her and the foundation she lives by…This emotion is desire…And this desire is to be with Shakeam. This is the very type of emotion she was conditioned never to have. Her gifts and abilities were not passed on to her for the purpose of self-gratification, but, for the good of the greater cause. Now, she wonders whether leaving G. W. behind was a good idea.

"Would you like to have something to drink?" Shakeam asks on his way to the kitchen. She decides to accompany him and is led into a room half the size of the other. The floor is smartly covered in cherry wood and cherry almond finished cabinets add to the modern, yet warmth of the room. She expected to see a quaint apartment-sized kitchen like Tom's and was pleasantly surprised to find something much larger. She runs an admiring hand over the stainless-steel door of the refrigerator and catches a glimpse of Shakeam staring at her from behind. He presses his warm body against hers. Her petite frame trembles as his warm body leans into hers and leaves no room for escape. She makes no attempt to loosen the firm grip while his arms gently guide her to turn towards him. Her body falls limp into his embrace as their lips meet. His mouth is moist and warm, firm, yet supple. His tongue parts her lips and, for the first time in her life, she experiences a kiss. In her mind, she has just become a woman, a real live human being. As far as she is concerned, there is no turning back. She's no longer a shapeshifter. She's no longer an alien. She's his woman now and forever.

G. W. IS STILL outside climbing to the top of the first wide cement step leading to the front door of the apartment building.

"This is taking too long," he complains aloud. "I've got to find a quicker way, and still remain unseen by these primitive human specimens."

He decides to make his body as straight as an arrow and propel himself over the remaining nine steps. He continues in flight until he reaches the revolving glass doors. With the force of both hands, he does a flip and successfully manages to push the revolving glass doors around.

"Whoa! Whoa!" he yells while holding onto the rotating door. "Plop!" he lands, headfirst, onto the marble lobby floor.

He sniffs the air for any signs of Cally and his nose leads him to the nearby elevators. While inside, he decides to push all the buttons with one swift leap. It turns out to be a good idea when her scent leads him to get off on the 4th floor.

G. W. doesn't anticipate being spotted by anyone. Even so, the squeal of a woman causes him to run for cover. He scrambles for cover behind the only visible object in sight, a potted floor plant.

"A mouse!" screams a robust, deep chocolate-skinned woman. "A filthy mouse!" she cries while looking up towards the frail mature gentleman accompanying her. "There. Over there! It came from the elevator!" she points.

"Out of the elevator?" the gentleman scoffs. "Since when do mice ride elevators my dear?" He calmly hands her a handkerchief while lovingly rubbing the middle of her back. "You say it ran towards that plant dear?" he questions. "Well, it won't hurt to take a look behind it for you."

The gentleman pulls the large pot forward and doesn't see any signs of a mouse or any other creature. Then, he slides a comforting arm around his companion's feigning waistline and escorts her onto the elevator.

"Now, sweetie, have you been taking your medication regularly?" he wonders.

"Oh, don't you talk to me about my medication. I know what I saw!" she snaps while stepping over the elevator threshold.

G. W. wipes the dirt from his brow with the back of one hand. Then, he cautiously jumps down from the pot and scurries down the hallway until Cally's scent dead ends at a door.

"This is it!" he confidently declares. G. W. presses an ear up to the door and listens for any detectable sounds of Cally. He hears voices.

"That's Cally!" he says aloud and is more determined than ever to find a way inside.

CHAPTER 20

LOVE WHISPERS

The word in the men's locker room about Laura is that she is a single mom. "You can have as many children as you want as long as they're all by me," Tom jokes while holding a snapshot of her close to his face.

He took a picture of Laura while at the last Company Christmas party. Tom was her Secret Santa last year and is so glad the candy apple red sweater looks great on her and is a perfect fit.

Suddenly, his head turns towards the sound of someone clearing their throat. It's Shakeam standing behind him with a shrewd look on his face.

"I couldn't help but notice whose picture you're holding," Shakeam says without hesitation. "Why don't you simply ask her out and tell her how you really feel? After all this time, she really needs to know. Don't you agree?"

Tom put the picture face down on his desk.

"I know, uh... I know," Tom stutters and tries to conceal his embarrassment by being agreeable.

"She does need to know," he concludes to himself. "Is she here today?"

Shakeam stretches his neck to see over the many cubicles strategically placed throughout the room.

"She is," he answers.

Tom runs a finger over the smoothness of the photo and admits to himself that Shakeam is one hundred percent correct in his assessment of their relationship. He tells himself that the charades must end here-and- now and concludes, Laura must know. Before Shakeam has a chance to say another word, Tom finds himself slowly drifting towards Laura's cubicle. The stickiness of the corner of the photo he's carrying is a clear indication that his palms are beginning to sweat. He stops by her workstation on a regular basis, he thinks, so, he is certain Laura won't find this visit out of the ordinary. Today, he decides, is the day to end this charade.

"Good morning!" she cheerfully greets and while he approaches, her eye moves down to the picture in his hand. "Oh! A picture…May I see it?"

Before Tom has a chance to respond, she snatches the photo out of his hand and stares at it in silence.

"This is a good photo," she tells him. "You had it all this time and didn't show it to me?" she pouts.

"Don't hate me for that," he tells her. "I'll make it up to you if you'll let me."

"What do you mean by that?" she wonders.

"Go out with me tonight or whenever," he tells her while kneeling on one knee and gently stroking her hand.

"You want to date me?" she sneers. "I mean, are you sure you want to date me?" she wants to know.

He rises to his feet, being careful not to break eye contact.

"Yes, I am sure," he answers.

She recognizes the seriousness in the tone of his voice and wants to end this conversation. She wants to change the subject, never to bring it up again. After all, she thinks, we have been friends forever and now he wants to upgrade our relationship to dating.

"I-I-I," she stammers while forcing a weak smile. "I don't know what to say…Are you serious?"

"Say no more," he says after sensing her awkwardness and decides to simply walk away.

"Wait…" she calls after him. "Meet me after work." Their eyes meet and without hesitation, he nods in agreement.

THROUGHOUT THE DAY, TIME drags on and he wonders whether this is going to be a date or simply a friendly excursion among old friends. I am the pursuer, and this means, he surmises, I must bring flowers. He thinks these won't be friendly flowers, like daffodils or tulips, but one dozen red roses should show her how I really feel.

Finally, it's evening and Laura eagerly prepares for her rendezvous with Tom. They're meeting for drinks at the hotel around the corner from work. Laura wishes she could go out on a real date; however, she concludes, drinks are better than nothing. She hasn't dated in three years and wants to make a good impression, even though her suitor is also her best friend.

Laura steps out of the taxi and quickly enters the hotel lobby. She's late and anxiously scanning the area for any signs of Tom. A large bouquet of red roses shields the face of the man just entering the building and heading in her direction. Laura's delighted to see that it's Tom.

"These are for you, of course," he says while thrusting the roses in her face.

"Thanks," gasps Laura. She instinctively blocks her face and pushes the roses away in the process.

Tom doesn't pay any attention to the thorns now sticking him in the chest. Laura notices, however, and decides to mention it after he gives her a warm kiss on the cheek.

"AREN'T YOU GOING TO pull those out?" she wonders.

Tom runs a hand over the front of his neatly pressed blue shirt.

"Ouch!" he complains after being stuck by one. His face turns red from embarrassment.

Here," she says while pulling them out one-by-one. "A thorn already stuck me in the hand, so, I know how it feels," she laughs. Her candor makes him comfortable enough to join in the laughter too.

"Care to join me?" he asks and extends an arm for her to hold while they walk to the hotel Bar Lounge.

Laura admires the roses and places them in a tall glass provided by the bartender. She tentatively listens as Tom talks about the job and points out the pros and cons of their workplace. As he talks and expresses himself with his hands, she wonders where this night may lead. Up until now, she's been comfortable with their 3-year relationship as friends. Even so, she is ready to make a commitment to someone for her 6-year-old daughter's sake as well as her own. She hates to admit it, but she is lonely and in need of a man in her life, not simply a friend.

"Thanks again for the roses," she tells him between sips of strawberry daiquiri. "They're beautiful and you didn't have to."

He leans towards her while sandwiching her hands between his.

"Thank me by going to dinner with me tonight and a movie," he says while studying her face for an answer.

"What time should I be ready?" she responds.

"Oh, I'll pick you up at 8," he tells her, then, as though it were second nature, Tom tenderly kisses her soft moistened lips.

"I'll see you at 8 then," she tells him.

At that moment, Laura notices a change in her thinking concerning Tom. Is he my friend, she wonders, or do I want him to be more? She keeps a watchful eye on him as he escorts her towards the hotel exit. Tom holds the door open for her, all the while whistling an upbeat tune. Listening to the joyful tune causes her to forget all about the nagging butterflies taking up residence inside her stomach. Suddenly, she has an epiphany and realizes he has all the positive attributes in a man she's been looking for.

CHAPTER 21

COSTUME BALL

The quest is to break up the monotony of their journey by doing something new and hopefully exciting. Terry dutifully calls the number found on the card she got from the man at the movie theater booth the other day. For Frank's sake, she gathers as much information as possible and soon finds out that the event will be held on a special night known as Halloween.

"Hello! Hello!" answers the man at the other end of the phone. His deep husky voice intimidates Terry at first. However, she quickly adapts to his style and sounds as rough and assertive as he does.

"Can you tell me how to get to the Costume Ball?" she shouts while holding the phone receiver with both hands.

The gentleman is silent for a moment.

"Hello?" she wonders. The crackling noise coming from the phone worries her that their connection may be severed. Suddenly, the voice returned.

"What side of town will you be coming from?" he asks.

"Hold on," she commands and drops the phone to the floor.

The confusion is clear to Frank and who sits on the edge of his seat. "What is it?" Frank impatiently wants to know.

In frustration, Terry throws her hands up into the air while pacing the floor.

"We need to know what side of town we're on before he can give us directions!" she whines.

Panicked, Frank yanks up the phone and yells into it.

"Hello! Hello!" he shouts. "Why can't you give us directions?" he snaps.

The voice remains surprisingly calm.

"Look Sir! Don't you know your own address?" He sincerely wants to know.

"Oh! Oh! Um! Well, I believe we can get that for you." Frank nervously assures the man then yells at Terry to search through Tom's mail for the address.

"Well," explains the man after being given the address. "The Ball is tonight and if you don't have your costumes by now, you won't be allowed in…I'm sorry."

Frank turns to Terry and smiles.

"Oh! No problem," Frank assures the man. "We're wearing our costumes right now."

THE BALL IS TONIGHT, thinks Frank, while pushing Terry to hurry with the ironing of their robes. The moon is full, and their guardians are all away on dates, he thinks while concluding that this is the perfect night for hunting.

Moments later, their newly laundered capes drape the ground at their feet while they slip out of the apartment unnoticed. Scampering through crowded streets towards the desired location, they are surprised by how close the hotel is. It's only about a 45-minute walk away.

"I heard somewhere that they serve lots of food at Balls," Terry says while wiggling her nose like a bunny ready to eat a carrot. Frank loves it when his spouse becomes excited. It always causes the hunter to surface inside of him even more. He is used to hunting to provide for his large family but now he can eat the bounty himself.

Soon thereafter, they enter the building and are met by a doorman dressed in a navy double-breasted suit, trimmed with red ribbing. Without an introduction, the man points them towards a hallway to the left, which leads into the Ballroom.

"I believe you two should go that way," he tells them while giving a nod of approval at their choice of costumes.

They step into a large room filled with chattering people. Most are dressed in elaborately feathered, extraterrestrial-looking costumes. People appear to be huddled in groups, drinking, laughing, and nibbling on finger food.

The trek fan from the theater spots them both standing in the doorway and makes his way through the crowd to greet them. Meanwhile, Frank and Terry are mesmerized by the splendor of the room and don't notice him. Their eyes look upward at the Chandeliers glistening and hanging from 14-foot ceilings. These splendid adornments sprinkle soft lighting throughout the ballroom. Birds sculpted out of ice take center-stage on the numerous elongated tables throughout the room. Along with the sculptors are a wide variety of fruits, cheeses, meats, and breads laid atop white tablecloths on each table.

Andy Crater, the man they met inside the movie theater lobby, is no stranger to sci-fi. The moment he catches up with them, he taps them on the shoulder and causes them to turn around.

"Oh! I remember you," Terry blushes then quickly turns to Frank. "He gave us this card, honey," she explains.

"You invited us!" she quickly says, then gives Andy a wide grin.

Andy slowly circles them once, then twice, and then, gives a reassuring nod of approval.

"And I'm so glad that I did. Cool!" He days with excitement. "As far as I'm concerned, you two deserve 1st place."

Andy takes Terry by the arm and escorts her into the crowd. She blushes and giggles in his ear. Andy is especially curious about the rock formations all over her skin. His hands work their way up and down the small of her back. There appears to be no end in sight to the formations, even so, he assures himself that they simply are good, very good at costuming.

"I bet you two are hungry," he assumes.

"You better believe it," replies Frank.

"You'll find food on all the tables with an ice sculpture. Just follow the birds and you'll feast like a king," he smiles, pats them both on their behinds, then disappears into the dense crowd.

An invitation to eat was all Frank needed to prove that all this sneaking around was worth it. Terry indulges along with him at every table and Frank nudges the happy partygoers aside to make room for them. They receive woos and aahs along the way and even double takes from some over the remarkable authenticity of their costumes.

CHAPTER 22
BARGING IN

G.W. is certain he has the strength to break down the door to get to Cally. He reasons, though, that as a visitor on this planet, adhering to protocol is the cardinal rule. It may appear a little odd when discovered, but, making a hole in the far-right corner of the door with his pocket laser is the most logical alternative.

Upon entering the apartment, G. W. follows the faint sound of voices. The sound leads him into a dimly lit room. Soft flowing music appears to float through the air from tiny boxes positioned throughout the l-shaped room. The place is smartly decorated, with lines, curves and a gray pallet of colors all complimenting each other. G. W. notices that the décor is a far cry from Tom's place, where a hodgepodge of furnishing was simply gathered and put into one small room. There, in the center of the largest sofa, sits Cally, uninhibited, wide-eyed, and so unlike G. W. had ever seen her before. To his surprise, Shakeam is kneeling on one knee before her and gently caressing her hands. "That's a precarious position," G. W. whispers to himself and wonders what Shakeam is up to. Then, he scurries to the far side of the room, being careful to remain close to the sofa she's sitting on.

"Will you marry me?" Shakeam asks.

G. W. is stunned-- no—he's flabbergasted-- no—he's shocked to hear such a question directed at Cally, a shapeshifter. Her girly smile sickens him so much so that his lips curl up to form a sinister grin.

"I-I-I don't know what to say," she stutters. Her mouth becomes unbearably dry. She attempts to swallow, but instead, gags and is forced to clear her throat.

"If only--" her voice quivers. "If only--"

Before she has the chance to finish her sentence, G. W., defying all gravity, leaps between the two of them and stands at attention. Cally scoots backwards and out of harm's way while Shakeam continues to kneel at her feet.

"So, you thought you could get away with this?" G. W. furiously snaps.

"Does he really know who you are?" G. W. yells. "Would he accept you whole-heartedly if he did?" he questions while completely ignoring the presence of a human.

She is crushed by the brutal truths of her reality. G. W. is right, she thinks. Just the same, the keyword she must take note of is truth. This is the truth. She's only a shadow passing through time. This humanbeing she cares for with all her heart and soul must never know who this shadow really is. While Shakeam rises to his feet she scans his immediate thoughts and discovers he believes G. W. to be a scientifically advanced talking doll.

"We don't have time for this," G. W. pauses and gives her the kind of mischievous grin that would surely draw suspicion in anyone's mind. "I never told you where Frank and Terry ran off to tonight."

She picks up on his urgency and quickly gathers her belongings on their way to the door.

"Ran off to where?" she wonders with apprehension. "You never told me they ran off-- period," she snaps while forcing him into her jacket pocket.

She looks back at her pursuer who finally decides to rise to his feet.

"Shakeam, I'm so sorry. I can't deal with this right now. Let's talk some other time," she tells him while whizzing out the door.

"Tell me about them," she crudely demands while struggling to run in high heels.

"So, now you want to know," he huffs with his arms neatly folded over his chest. "And here you are, an Ambassador from the Nebula, off on some romantic interlude while your colleagues explore the world all by themselves. They're all by themselves," he chides. "So, do you really care to know?" he taunts.

"I've had enough of this," she assures him through clinched teeth. "What do you want me to do? Admit that I've been wrong?" she pleads.

A sinister grin rises over his face. As far as he can recall, she's never admitted being wrong about anything.

"Okay!" she cowards. "I admit it! I was wrong," she concedes. "Now, where are they?" she demands while blaming herself for this mishap as much as he does.

CHAPTER 23

THE CHASE

Andy gently leads Terry away from the table in hopes that Frank will follow. An insatiable appetite has carried him from table-to-table tearing into the delicacies like a starved wild boar. To his shame, he has drawn the attention of everyone at the Ballroom and will soon attract hotel security.

Andy leads her past the crowds to a short well-lit corridor. It is elegantly adorned with paintings hung on walls and pricey artifacts are displayed atop white marbled pedestals. While glancing back, he is relieved to see Frank reluctantly trailing behind. Frank closes in on Andy and Terry studying the painting of a small child romping through an array of colorful flowers.

"I've been meaning to ask you two where you're from," Andy says. "I mean…" he hesitates and props his hands on his hips. "Tell me that that display, that eating frenzy, was all a part of the act?"

Terry and Frank's eyes meet. They're confused by the question.

"What do you mean?" asks Terry while evading his piercing gaze. She hopes he'll quit while he's ahead and not pry any longer. After all, they really did attend this event for the sole purpose of eating, so, she wonders who in their right minds could ever find fought in them for that.

Andy scratches his forehead. A nervous habit he picked up as a teen when faced with peer pressure.

"Come on guys…I told a few people here that I invited you two. Now, if you show-out like two pigs-in-a-blanket, you won't be invited to anymore of these gigs and I won't be able to show my face for years," he moans.

Frank can be very defensive about his eating rituals. When it's eating time, he does not intend to hold back for anyone. He especially won't hold back for this human whom he most likely will never lay eyes on again. With a force unlike Andy has ever experienced before, a hand grabs hold of his collar and lifts him off the ground.

"Listen human!" Frank angrily warns. "We just came to your social event for substance, nothing more. Do not hinder our feeding again!" he growls.

Terry gives Frank a disturbed wait-until-I-get-you-home look causing him to abruptly drop Andy. Terry scoops Andy up into her arms before he hits the white and gray marbled floor. At that moment, Andy realizes this couple is The Real McCoy. They look too real and too authentic not to be real and authentic, he reasons. He imagines all the awesome adventures they must have been on and how he'd love to take them to the next sci-fi conference. He grabs them both by the hands and shakes with great enthusiasm.

"You two stay right here!" he insists, then, disappears into the crowd of partygoers. When he returns with his friends, they're gone from the quiet corner he left them in.

"Fritz!" he curses. "I'm not leaving here without pictures and proof they're not from earth!" he tells Raymond, his closest friend. Determined to find them, he roams from room-to-room, from buffet table to buffet table until he catches them drawing a crowd once again.

Frank comfortably squats on top of a table next to an Ice Sculpture, fearlessly devouring the food around him. His beastly snorting appears to appeal to the onlookers. Some clap and cheer at his performance. Terry, on the other hand, is not eating at all for fear of the crowd closing in around them. She doesn't like being pinned into a corner and doesn't feel comfortable putting her eating habits on display for all to gawk at.

"It's time to leave," she nervously tells Frank.

Andy moves in closer, pushing his way through the thick crowd of onlookers. He snaps picture-after-picture while circling his subjects. He climbs onto the table and snaps the cell phone camera directly in Franks face. The flash momentarily blinds Frank. His head rises at the intrusion,

and he bats his eyes, wipes his snout with the back of his hand, then continues to indulge. He would've feasted all night had it not been for the constant pleas from his spouse. He leaps down from the table onto all fours and hisses and growls at the constant flashes coming from Andy's camera. Andy posts pictures on his Facebook page and watches the event go viral while Frank and Terry escape together, far away from the hoopla and the flashes of the annoying camera. They inadvertently slip into an unfamiliar room and find themselves in a hidden garden full of a wide variety of plants and trees.

The herbal scent flowing from a diversity of plant life and vegetation overwhelms their senses.

"Live prey!" they both declare after hearing the chatter of birds.

Frank wonders why Andy never told them about this exquisite room. Birds of every shape, size, and origin imaginable sing a long shrill of alarm while fluttering from tree-to-tree and from plant-to-plant. The room reminds them of Prehisteria, their home world, where the nights are long and the light from the two moons always makes the conditions ripe for hunters like themselves. For Lizaradactiles, the thrill of the hunt is as intoxicating and as gratifying as the feast itself. So, now, Frank mounts up onto all four limbs in preparation for another hunt.

He spies on his first target, a pair of yellow finches with deep blue masks and orange beaks. Defying all laws of gravity, his wings extend far beyond the length of his firm body. One swift motion of his strong legs thrust him into mid-air. With the veracity of a shark and the tenacity of a bulldog, he chomps down on his prey. Feathers fly in every direction while the second finch escapes, but not for long. He leaps, flies, and leaps again from tree-to-tree and limb-to-limb until he corners his next victim. He lassos it with his elongated tongue and gulps it down within seconds. Frank quickly scans the room for more prey and sees his mate picking a feather out of her teeth while standing on the thick branch of a tree a few yards away. Terry turns to him and has a thin smile of satisfaction pasted across her face.

CHAPTER 24

ATRIUM PREY

As Cally moves through the city towards the Costume Ball location, G. W. can feel the pulsation of her blood flowing through each vein. She races past shops, skyscrapers, and restaurants, all of which are a blur to the natural eye.

"Hey!" yells G. W. "You wouldn't have to do this had you listened to me in the first place!"

She blows out a sigh, then, reaches towards her side pocket to force his head back inside.

"You can't hide from the truth!" his muffled voice badgers.

THE DISTINCTIVE ODOR OF the Lizaradactiles leaves a trail in the air that Cally quickly picks up. Like a sleepwalker, she is duty bound to follow her nose which leads to an upscale hotel. The moment she walks over the threshold, the white and gold marble floors accented by dazzling chandelier laden ceilings, distract her for a moment. She hasn't seen such exquisitely beautiful floors since living in the Nebula. A quick scan of the room is all she needs to pick up the trail again. Her nose leads them to a large room with high ceilings riveted with shimmering crystal chandeliers. Patrons dressed in colorful, flamboyant costumes whiz by her while carrying wine glasses filled with bubbling Champaign cocktails. The plaque over the wide double-door entrance reads Ballroom A. In the midst of the gala affair, she soon discovers that Frank and Terry could easily blend into this assembly unnoticed. Her senses reveal that there was once an orderly array of food meticulously arranged on top of each table lining the walls of the room. Now, all that remains is a few morsels of cheese, scattered bits of fruit, and other unrecognizable hors d'oeuvres. She is certain now that Frank and Terry ventured into this room and raised a ruckus like no one on this planet has ever witnessed before.

G. W. decides to wiggle his way to the top of the backpack to peer around the room.

"Are these all visitors too?" he wonders aloud.

"Back in the bag," she orders. "We don't want to have to explain you. Now do we?"

The moment G. W. reluctantly dives for cover and recalls the reason for Frank and Terry being here. They were invited to a Halloween Ball. How could he forget, he wonders?

Cally ignores all the partying going on around her to concentrate on her nose. Before she has the chance to take another step though, a costume wearing partygoer commandeers her by the waist.

"Let's dance baby!" he orders while drawing her body towards his.

His breath reeks of liquor and summer sausage and although she tries to break free like a normal human female her size would, every attempt proves to be futile. Cally gives-in for now by swaying back and forth with the uncouth stranger who has forest green skin. The stranger has taken the form of a green creature she once knew on planet Mars, only, she didn't have pale hands like he does.

"Excuse me," Cally tells the green stranger while using all her natural strength to push him away again. "I need to go," she explains apologetically.

He thanks her for the brief dance, then, takes off his mask which reveals that he is human. Though his face is pale, his physique reminds her of Shakeam. Shakeam is mine, she thinks. Cally shakes her head at the thought of someone being hers. She tells herself being with him is impossible, and quickly puts the thought behind her.

"About time!" snaps G. W. about the dance partner. "The next time we come to earth, you need to take on a less appealing form," he huffs.

She inwardly agrees.

They notice a crowd is gathering at the arched glass doors leading to the Atrium. Onlookers intently watch in amazement so; Cally moves towards them for a closer look. Being certain the Lizaradactiles are in the Atrium, she pushes her way through the crowd and slips through the doorway.

"I wouldn't go in there if I were you," a young woman wearing antennas on a black skull cap warns.

"Yea, something weird is happening in there," a youthful man using binoculars for eyes agrees.

Despite their warnings, she follows her nose into the Atrium and is suddenly startled by the sound of sirens blaring just outside. In the middle of impending danger, she remains helpless as long as she is in this fragile human form. A flock of birds suddenly take flight and all fly towards her as though they sense she is the only one capable of rescuing them. Cally ducks down moments before Frank leaps out from behind a huge banana tree, and flies towards the birds in flight. Not far behind, Terry waddles on foot with a yellow and blue feather sticking out from one corner of her mouth. It's not difficult for Cally to conclude that their predator instincts have completely taken control. They are on the kind of feeding frenzy she warned Tom about. Her only recourse is to subdue them by force, even in the sight of onlookers. G. W. is aware of her dilemma and decides to act by climbing down from her shoulder and disappearing into the thick of the trees.

"What are you doing!" she yells at the Lizaradactiles, then, quickly realizes it's too late to stop them from leaping out of sight. Faint whispers of their voices guide her to them. G. W. perches on a tree limb and mimics the chirping of birds to lure Frank and Terry away from the prey as well as out of sight of the crowd.

"Now…Do your thing!" he commands. Cally nods in appreciation and quickly assumes the menacing form of a prehistoric Mastodon. It stands a full 12 feet, towering over the tropical plants surrounding them. An extended trunk slaps both Lizaradactiles causing them to stagger to the ground. After Frank and Terry regain their composure and struggle to their feet, they belch to attention.

"What's that noise?" Terry wonders at the cries of police sirens.

"There must be a way back out," panics Cally after assuming her pleasing human form once again.

"I'll make a way!" G. W. assertively declares. He motions for everyone to step away from the wall behind them and to everyone's surprise he begins spinning like a toy top. G. W.'s spinning startles Frank and Terry out of the state of euphoria caused by eating raw flesh. The wall shakes violently, then sways back and forth until it crumbles and makes a hole the size of a door. Dazed by the recent events, they file one-by-one out of the room and into a deserted alley.

The recent rain has caused the streets to glisten, so getting home before the streets freeze over is a major concern now.

The aliens watchfully round the corner and endeavor to blend in with the stirring crowd surrounding the front of the hotel. Cally has no problem maneuvering around loitering pedestrians but becomes apprehensive at the sight of the police.

"Oh! There is a masquerade ball up the street," Cally lies to a couple staring at Frank and Terry. "We just left there," she explains before disappearing into the crowd ahead.

After traveling for at least 4 blocks, Cally senses there is no one shadowing them. While she stretches her strides to make up for lost time, Frank and Terry purposely lag in search of more live prey.

"Get back over here…You scoundrels!" G. W. orders while keeping a watchful eye on them. "The path is this way," he scolds and motions with one arm for them to follow.

"This has got to stop!" snaps Cally. "Is this the only reason why I'm here?" she angrily huffs. "Is it to babysit you two day and night?"

No one responds to her rhetoric. Especially not Frank and Terry, who are behaving rather lethargic and out-of-touch with their surroundings. The ecstasy of the feeding-frenzy is wearing off even though they don't ever wish it to leave. Both are well-pleased with the thrill of their quest since they now have a story to tell the Lizaradactiles back in Prehisteria. They are proud to be able to share their adventures with their children and clan. Predators must always reinforce their self-worth by capturing prey. Being cooped up in that one-bedroom apartment day-in and day-out began to drain their zeal for life. The thrill of the hunt has rejuvenated them. So now, they will stand before the Council with pride and confidence. Nothing anyone says or does to them will take that pride away, not even Cally's snide remarks or her overbearing actions.

As they draw nearer to Tom's apartment, G. W.'s internal alarm turns on. Only he can hear it though and only he can communicate with the caller.

"Ambassador, Honorable Ambassador," speaks the caller. "You are the first to know and must take action to protect humans right away," the caller anxiously alerts.

"I am the first to know what?" G. W. wonders.

"The war has begun," the caller tells him. "Those who once were the light of the universes have now joined forces to fight against Ishi (God of all) and all that is good, including the humans. You must prepare them," he pleads. "Please, I implore you. You must stay and prepare…"

The transmission abruptly ends in static. He peeps out of the backpack and is relieved to see the building Tom lives in is only a few feet away.

Later that night, while everyone else was asleep, he decided to contact the Council. He no longer reports to the enemies of the Council. They were the Council Members who pushed for him to come on this mission. Instead, he decides to devise a plan of action to take to ward off this invasion against planet Earth. Above all else, he wants humans to live.

CHAPTER 25

MORE THAN FRIENDS

Tom looks at his wristwatch just as the Uber driver pulls up to the curb and he notices it is exactly 8pm. "Good job Kaleem", he says while handing the driver a generous tip.

Tom slides both hands down the sides of his white cotton-blend shirt. Too much moisture on his hands is a sure sign of nervousness and he doesn't want Laura to peg him for having cold, clammy hands. He's wanted a date with Laura for over two years. Now that the opportunity has arrived, he's determined to put his best foot forward. "Look for the third door on the right once you get to the third floor," he tells himself aloud while stepping into the gold-plated elevator.

When the elevator stops on the third floor, Laura's directions lead him directly to her door. The modern fan-top sconces used for lighting the long hallway, cast a soft spotlight over the numbers etched on the doors. Tom knocks until he hears the soft voice of a child on the other side of the door.

Laura escorts her six-year-old daughter, Aylia, to the five-piece glass-topped dinette located in the far corner of the eat-in kitchen. The child's meal is meticulously arranged on a pastel green placemat covered in pink philodendrons. The linen placemat, which matches the rest of the décor in the narrow L-shaped kitchen, reminds Laura of her favorite time of year, springtime.

"You sit here…" she tells Aylia and gently kisses her on the forehead. "…And eat your dinner. It's about time for our guest to arrive. You're going to excuse yourself and go to your room after I introduce you to him. Okay baby?" Aylia smiles and quickly nods before climbing onto the tan broadcloth covered dinette chair.

"Am I going to get a new Daddy?" she innocently wonders.

Laura bends down and kisses her on the cheek again.

"No baby. You'll always only have one Daddy and he's in heaven right now."

Laura glances at the memorial she made for her late husband, which is in the hallway adjacent to the kitchen. For three years she has had a candle burning in front of the various pictures of him. Something died inside of her the day she heard the awful news that Wilson, her husband, had been involved in a fatal traffic accident and would not be coming home. The shock of the news sent her into a year- long depression. She lost the will to live and was hospitalized for most of that time, but for Aylia's sake she gave life another chance. Now, she wonders if she will be able to give love another try?

Tom's hands prepare to knock again and this time he follows through by pushing all fears aside. To his surprise, the door swings wide open and the beauty of his attractive date literally takes his breath away. She notices the deep gulp, then, the clearing of his throat, and is pleasantly flattered by his interest in her. Laura is uncharacteristically enchanted by his presence and displays it with a warm, quick kiss to his cheek.

"Come in," she invites while pulling the door open and forcing it shut with one hand. She struggles with the lock, so, Tom reaches from behind, places his hand over hers, and steadies the door. She quickly locks it and is afraid she'll lose her composure too soon in the game if she exhales now.

The pleasurable scent of her perfume sends waves of desire through Tom's body. He wants this moment to last longer, but being the gentleman he is, he steps back as soon as she turns her full-figured body away from the door. Their gazes meet and Tom looks deep into her hazel eyes where flickers of light from nearby candles enhance their beauty.

With the wave of a hand, she ushers him into the foyer. He follows her lead and scans the apartment layout from the foyer. "I love your apartment," he smiles while practically walking on her heels.

"Thanks. I'd love it too if I had a second bedroom," she smartly replies.

He follows her around the corner through a narrow foyer into the living room while checking out the royal blue chiffon t-strapped dress clinging to a shapely hourglass figure.

As she walks in front of him, he lingers behind to admire the way her t-strapped two and a half-inch heel accent the sexy curves in her legs.

"Have a seat," she beckons with the wave of a hand. Tom sinks down onto the pillowed sofa cushions which are covered in ocean blue suede cloth.

"I just need to check on my daughter, Aylia," she tells him, all the while, studying his face for a reaction. She has decided that anyone who dates her will have to accept her child wholeheartedly.

"Oh! You have a daughter?" His voice sounds strained. The news momentarily takes his breath away. He had no idea she had a daughter. They'd known each other for three years and she never said a word about a child.

Laura escapes to the next room, not expecting him to trail behind. Tom follows though and stops at the memorial in the hallway. He bends down to take a closer look at the one lit candle surrounded by pictures of a handsome young man about his age. He suddenly feels insignificant and threatened by the sight of another man in her apartment, even though he is only in the pictures. Who is this man, he wonders? Is he still a part of her life? He studies the setting a little further to understand the meaning of it all and concludes that it is obviously a memorial of some kind. "Oh crap", he worries aloud, he'll have to compete with a martyr. His hand quickly covers his mouth at the sound of the sweet squeaky voice of a child.

The kitchen is small and darkened with dark oak finished cabinets and a floor way too dark for his taste. He moves closer to the child seated at the glass dinette. It surprises him when Laura slides her hand into his.

"Aylia," she pauses. "This is Tom."

Tom gracefully bows before the child.

"It's a pleasure to meet you little princess," he smiles. "Hum…" he says while holding a hand behind his ear. "I thought I heard someone say you are a Princess. Are you a Princess?"

Her gentle round face blushes to a rosy red. Then, she buries her face into her mother's dress. Hazel brown eyes glance up at Laura and she whispers, "Momma, I like him. Is he going to spend the night with us?"

"No," Laura squirms and blushes. "Don't you have something else to do right now, baby?"

Aylia looks up at Tom. "Mommy wants me to excuse myself and go to bed now, but I won't really be asleep," she lets him know.

"Okay baby you can tell Tom goodnight," her mom orders.

"Goodnight," says Aylia.

"Goodnight," replies Tom. "Nice meeting you."

Laura exhales after she finally gets Aylia to go to sleep. This is her first date in over three years, and she doesn't want her baby to walk in on something she shouldn't see at her tender age.

"She's adorable. How old is she?" he asks.

"Oh… she's 6 going on 16," she laughs.

"Would you like red wine with the meal?" she wants to know.

"I don't know. It depends on all we're having," he responds.

"Silly me," she smirks. "I hope you like Italian! We're having chicken parmesan over pasta along with fresh bread sticks and Caesar salad."

"Yum…" Tom smiles. "Red wine would be great!"

After the meal, Tom stays in the kitchen and ignores Laura's wishes for him to relax in the living room. She wants to leave the dishes for later and enjoy the evening alone with him now.

"Sit down," he demands while grabbing a chair and pushing it beneath her legs. "Sit!" he orders, then, gently pushes down on her shoulders until she complies. "A meal like that deserves a reward, so, the first thing I'm going to do for you is clean up the kitchen."

"No, no!" she stands to her feet in protest.

"Yes…indeed," he insists and takes the fight out of her by grabbing her around the waist and firmly pressing his lips against hers. Laura staggers back to the table while breathing heavily. He grabs her again, this time kissing her with more passion than before until she pushes him away.

"Will you allow me to do the dishes now?" he wants to know with the sexiest smile she has ever seen on a man.

"Will you stop kissing me?" she politely asks.

"If that's what you want?" he replies. "Is it?"

"For now, let's just take it slow," she says while clearing her throat. Laura is amazed at how much Tom's kisses remind her of Wilson. I never thought I'd find another man who would be able to out kiss my late husband, she smiles, but Tom has beat him, hands-down. Laura sighs in contentment while watching Tom bust suds in her kitchen sink.

CHAPTER 26

BROKEN RULES

Tom returns home from his date with Laura to a quiet apartment. One thing Tom has always been able to count on is the TV blasting whenever Frank and Terry are around. Tonight, however, there is no noise from the TV. There are no lights turned on. And a quick glance into the refrigerator confirms that something is out of place. It is full of food and Tom is certain that this is odd, even for them. It has been the cardinal rule for the visitors to clear that fridge out every evening before Tom gets home. This way he can do an inventory of supplies needed and pick them up the following day. Now, it is just as full as it was when he left this morning. No one is resting in his bedroom. No one is hanging from the coat rack in the closet. And further observations reveal that no one is in the bathroom or on the patio. His heart races at the thought of the Aliens being in danger again. Tom wonders where they all could be at 2am in the morning.

"CALM DOWN," TOM CONSOLES himself while pacing the floor. "It will be all right." He assures himself that they are okay. "I will find them," he declares. "They wouldn't just leave like this without good reason."

His hand unconsciously reaches for the TV remote and clicks the TV on.

"Our top story today is a bit of a mystery," the newscaster says with a smile. "A couple dressed like aliens apparently crashed a costume party for the sole purpose of eating all the food--literally. One picture is worth a thousand words, so--watch this video donated by an onlooker at the scene."

The video showed the so-called aliens on top of a long serving table savagely devouring food. The next scene revealed the same couple's incredible flight through mid-air in pursuit of the Hotel's rarest bird collection.

"Now that's what I call a true Halloween party," the news woman chuckles.

"The number…!" Tom yells into the phone. "Give me the number to the Costume Ball hotel!"

"Hello…I'm calling to find out what happened to those creatures that ate up all the food," Tom demands. There is a moment of silence on the other end of the receiver.

"Well, Sir. What did you say your name was?" he slyly inquires. It's no surprise to Tom that the man is suspicious. Even so, he presses the man for more information.

"I just want to come down to take a few pictures," Tom fabricates.

"Aah…Another reporter…Well-- you're too late. Somehow, they were able to sneak out with a honey-of-a-woman. No one even saw them leave. It was spooky you know," the hotel clerk explains until Tom abruptly ends the conversation by slamming down the receiver.

"Where could they be?" he wonders aloud.

Suddenly, there is a faint knock at the door, so, Tom tiptoes towards it and squints through the peephole. To his surprise, he sees Cally, Frank and Terry huddled together in the hallway. Without giving it another thought, he yanks the door open, causing the three of them to tumble into the foyer. Cally scrambles to her feet while Frank and Terry roll over onto their knees. Tom is so happy to see them that he can't seem to stop kissing Cally all over her head, neck and even her arms. Then, Terry pushes Cally aside to get in on the kissing action and puckers her lips for Tom to kiss too.

"I just saw you and Frank on the news," he says while politely pushing Terry to the side. "What were you thinking?"

"All I can say is that I'm sorry. I'm sorry for them. "I'm sorry for myself and Shakeam. I'm sorry for everything," cries Cally before running to the bathroom and locking herself in.

Meanwhile, G. W. climbs out of the discarded backpack and jumps onto the coffee table.

"Well old man," he says while peering up at Tom. "That was different." He's referring to Cally's outburst. None of them ever thought it possible for her to have a meltdown like that one.

Tom is at a loss for words.

"It's time to get some shut eye, my friend," Tom says to G. W. who follows Tom to the bedroom.

After her associates settle in for the night, Cally sits on the edge of the tub wondering how to tactfully break the news of their departure to Tom. She feels they have overstayed their welcome and have done more harm than good. She will be grateful to Tom forever for his generosity and compassion towards them all. He will be missed, she concludes. However, the matters troubling her more than anything are her feelings for Shakeam. The observer never becomes personally involved with the test subjects. Cally has crossed that line and fears she may never see him again unless she does the unthinkable. The only practicable solution is to leave this planet and she has decided to inform them all of her decision first thing in the morning.

While nestled in the makeshift bed in Tom's dresser, G. W. anticipates great danger coming to the earth. The humans are not prepared for the possible attack from the Galactic rebels. As a double agent, he has learned their plan and must reveal their diabolical intentions to the Council leaders. He knows that these sly creatures will join forces and send down an invisible army for the purpose of possessing every living soul. They become whomever they possess. They feed off the pain, misery, and suffering of others and they are lovers of chaos and mayhem. He knows he must sound the alarm and replay his messages to the Council. Consequently, they will have to devise a plan to stop the invasion or at least postpone it until the earthlings evolves enough to resist such an attack on its own. This is the law of the Universe.

CHAPTER 27

UNDER INVESTIGATION

Andy Bordeaux, the young man first contacted by Frank, receives an unexpected visit from Detective Allen Dodson and his wing man, Hall Wade. Dodson is assigned by the local authorities to investigate the two mysterious guests who attended the Costume Ball.

"I first met them at a late-night movie. It was weird man, but Kool at the same time," Andy tells the detective. "I told them they'd win first place at the Halloween Ball, and I was right," he recounts the events while grinning from ear to ear. "Can I pick'em or can I pick'em," he boasts while sticking out his chest.

"Did they tell you where they are from?" the detective probs.

"Why-- Are they here? And who could've predicted they were real aliens!" Andy exclaims while rocking back and forth in the metal chair.

The detectives leave without knowing any more now than they did when they first arrived.

"He's on something," Dodson tells his partner while getting into the car. "Imagine that" Wade snidely agrees, all the while, being facetious. They leave Andy's place to investigate their next lead. "Aliens!" they scoff.

"Hey man— Who's next on our list?" asks Dodson.

"The place where the call originated is the next lead. The directory tells us the address and the apartment are rented by a Tom Clancey," he squints while reading it on his iPad.

"Map that address and let's pay this joker a visit," Detective Dodson orders.

CHAPTER 20

PACK TO GO

Cally holds back tears while looking down at the few items she and her colleagues brought with them to earth. She stuffs it all into the lone backpack they share and impatiently waits at the apartment door for the others. Today is the day she insisted they all leave planet earth. Given the circumstances surrounding the fiasco at the Halloween party, she feels they all have no choice except to depart.

Thoughts of Shakeam cause her eyes to tear up. A thin stream of salty tears flows down the sides of her cheeks. Cally has never experienced this side of human emotions before, and it frightens her. She shudders at the possibility of being trapped inside this human visage forever. Nevertheless, this is exactly what could happen if she were to choose loving this human over civic duty as Ambassador to earth. Cally realizes she must set aside all personal feelings for this human. "I can't do it," she whispers.

In the living room, Frank amuses Terry with loud, hardy burps. Terry responds with earsplitting laughter and draws everybody's attention away from packing.

"Time to go everyone," Cally announces. "It's been fun," she facetiously says, "But…we've got to go now."

G. W. leaps onto Cally's shoulder and nestles into the outer pocket of the backpack.

"Did you think I was going to fly myself to the rendezvous sight, hum?" he chides. She shakes her head from side to side at his comment and realizes this is simply his way of getting attention.

"I'll miss you too," she tells him and soon afterwards embraces Tom, and they say their tearful good-byes as well.

"You will be missed too my friend," Frank tells him. The sight of all four aliens leaving causes Tom more sorrow than he ever could've imagined. They have become his family, and he fears he may never lay eyes on them again.

"I don't feel comfortable allowing you all to be left alone in the middle of the night like this. It's just not safe," his voice quivers.

Tom's tears flow down his cheeks as he reaches towards them for a group hug. Cally wipes a tear away from her cheek; Frank clears his throat; Terry begins to wail; as her custom is, and G. W. quietly sighs. Despite the tug at their hearts, the urgency to leave is stronger than ever.

G. W. tells Tom, "You've been more than an adequate host and a genuine friend as well. I will miss you, pal."

G. W. wishes he could share with Tom the news about the imminent danger coming to the earth. Then, he reasons, it won't do him any good to know about such matters. He will, however, persuade the Council to protect the earth at all costs. The opportunity to form a bond with real humans is priceless. Now, they are far more than simply statistics in his memory banks, they are his friends and worth saving.

The other visitors feel the same way about Tom as G. W. does. They all feel like Tom has become more than an assignment, he's, their friend.

"Same here," Frank says before slapping Tom on the back and Terry nods in agreement.

More tears roll down Cally's cheeks and she is puzzled about not being able to stop the flow.

"You showed me the nature of human love. We all believed, up until now, that only Ishi possesses true love that can touch a heart," she tells him. "Now, we know that humans possess the power to carry and distribute love from the heart as well. Tell Shakeam I will always care deeply for him and will treasure the little time we spent together, forever."

CHAPTER 29

GONE HOME

Cally leads the way at a merciless pace towards their destination. Occasionally, she glances back at Frank and Terry and is astonished by the way they are nipping at her heels. She must conclude, they are as anxious to leave earth as she is. Anyway, she is pleased they haven't voiced one iota of a complaint about her ferocious pace.

She locates their ship, which is only a few yards away, and nearly trips over the pint size barking dog approaching her with a vengeance.

"Shoos!" She commands and uses one hand to beat it to the side.

"Get back, you fowl beast!" snaps Frank.

"Be nice little cutie!" Terry says.

It nips at Frank and Terry's heels. Then, it growls and sniffs while encircling them. Frank instinctively scoops up the fury brown creature with the intent of consuming a quick meal.

"Release it," Cally sternly orders while moving towards him and squeezing him by the shoulders. Frank lets go and the dog falls to the ground. Despite them quieting the dog, he shakes himself and continues to bark as much as before.

"I'm sure it will be missed by someone," she shouts, then, renders the dog and all within ear shot of them, motionless.

All life about them is eerily silent. Even the cries of the crickets have ceased to exist. They're in a time warp and literally, within the blink of an eye, Cally and her friends will be gone. She presses the button on the band around her wrist that was cleverly designed to look like an ordinary wristwatch. The stabilizer unlocks with the single touch of a button and their transportation suddenly appears. A butter yellow hue surrounds the borders of the diamond shaped vessel, and the stairs quickly unfold before them from the bottom of the craft. They all board and take their appointed positions in the ship's control center. Immediately, their spacecraft descends into the heavens far above the earth.

CHAPTER 30

LONELY NEST

I t feels good to have his sofa back, even though the place feels unbearably empty. Tom assures himself that he'll adjust to the peace and quiet of the humble abode once again. However, he wonders about the fate that may fall upon the world as the result of this brief encounter. I didn't dare pose these questions to the visitors; he thinks while recalling Grandfather Bert's explicit warning not to pry. Grandfather Bert instructed Tom to simply act as their host and liaison--nothing more. Tom followed these explicit instructions because he did not want to risk having the privilege transferred to another family. If that were to happen, the honor of ambassadorship would be lost forever to his lineage.

A sudden rapping at the door interrupts his train of thoughts. Tom checks the time and it's 6 am.

"Who is it? What do you want?" Tom demands while dreading who could possibly be at his door at this early hour. Tom concludes, it must be the four ambassadors and snatches open the door.

"Tom, Tom Clancy?" the man in a gray suit says his name as a question.

Tom quickly responds, "Yes!" while thinking something terrible must have happened to his friends.

"May we come in…Sir?" the other somber man asks.

"Who are we-e-e?" Tom warily inquires.

"Oh…well…allow me to introduce myself," the older gentleman astutely answers. "I'm Detective Dodson of the Denver Police Department and this is my partner Detective Wade."

He quickly parades a badge beneath Tom's nose and steps over the threshold.

"What's this all about?" Tom nervously wants to know while waving them into his quaint living room.

"Have a seat young man. We're just here to ask a few questions about your guests," Dodson tells him as he sits down directly across from him.

"Yes…Sit," Wade concurs. "You don't have to be nervous around us. We're your friends."

Tom suspects that these two men don't have a clue about the identity of his alien visitors, and he intends to keep it that way.

"We've been trying to solve a mystery," Wade bluntly tells him.

"Hold on here…I'll handle this," huffs Dodson. "I'm the lead detective here…Remember?"

"Oh…Of course," Wade cowards.

"Did you or your friends or anyone you know of, attend a costume party yesterday evening?" Dodson continues the questioning.

"Well…" Tom pauses. "No-- I don't think so," he responds in a firm and resolute manner.

"What do you mean…You don't think so? Aren't you sure?" he drills. "Do you live alone or not? How many people live here with you? May we search the apartment?"

As a cobra raises its curious head to attack, Dodson follows Tom's every move. He inches forward to make eye-to-eye contact and reasons, if this doesn't intimidate him into talking, nothing will.

Tom's excessive blinking annoys Dodson to no end and compels the detective to dig for the truth even further.

"Where do you work? Can your answers be verified and with whom?"

Finally, after more than an hour of grueling questioning, the detective takes a coffee break by helping himself to the espresso machine in the kitchen.

While the coffee brews, Tom comes up with a way to clear his good name. He jumps to his feet and declares:

"Yes, I did have someone living with me for a few days. They are long gone by now. I know about the costume party; however, I did not attend myself. I found out about it, after the fact, while watching the late-night news. What's this all about?" Tom forcefully questions.

Their deafening silence disturbs Tom. However, he can't help but to be amused by the cock-eyed expressions being made by the so-called lead detective. His dark brown eyes blink nonstop behind black horn-rimmed glasses. Tom is taken aback by the way this detective swirls his ball point pen like a baton through long mannish fingers. It's his trademark and everyone he has ever worked with considers his repertoire to be somewhat quirky. It's Dodson's version of pacing the floor or doodling on a notepad whenever a person gets stumped on a case. Now though, Dodson is worried that clearing this guy will send them back to square one, meaning no leads.

"Tell me about your friends?" Dodson persists.

Cally sensed that the Authorities were hot on their trail, so this must have been her reason for abruptly leaving. Tom's not upset with her decision. He only hopes and prays they made it to their spacecraft unharmed.

"They were my cousins," he explains. "They were here on vacation," he pauses to piece together the words. "You know…trying to have a good time."

The hour hand on the wall clock whizzes by with each wary question. Tom sighs after taking a winded deep breath and with each waking moment grows wearier of his interrogators.

"As I mentioned before--" he hastily explains. "They left already to return to their homes and, no, I don't know where home is," he sighs realizing he just incriminated himself. Naturally, he thinks everyone knows where their relatives live if they come for an extended visit. I need a lawyer…he fears…I need Shakeam.

CHAPTER 31

WINDING DOWN

Morning arrives too soon for Tom. It feels like he just laid down a few minutes ago. Of course, the late departure of the visitors and the unexpected, early morning, visit from the detectives left little time for sleep. He turns over to silence the snooze for the fourth time and, in a panic, hurls himself into the shower and literally dresses on his way out the door.

To his dismay, at work Shakeam greets him at the main entrance of the building and hastily shuttles him into his corner office.

"We have to talk," Shakeam insists while sitting his briefcase aside and reaching for a pack of his favorite cappuccino. He plops the pack into the Coreg coffeemaker, then, turns his full attention to Tom.

"I hope I'm not imposing," Shakeam apologetically tells him. "But I have to—correction--I need information from you about your cousin." The puzzled look on Tom's face is unsettling for Shakeam.

Tom absentmindedly blanks out the pretend cousin he introduced to his boss and looks at Shakeam like he's crazy.

"Cally!" he says, raising his voice an octave. "You know… honey-brown… drop-dead gorgeous!"

Tom finally gets the connection and furthers his pretense.

"Oh yes…that cousin. What would you like to know?" Tom casually responds.

That's the in-the-know look Shakeam was expecting in the first place. He leaps from his comfortable chair to confront Tom face-to-face.

"Where is she?" Shakeam is losing his normal calming mannerism and coming loose at the seams. "I've been trying to reach her all morning. I asked her to marry me, and I won't take no for an answer," he bellows while wiping the sweat from his brow.

Tom belches out a cough to conceal the wave of unpleasant emotions swelling inside of him.

"Are you okay buddy," Shakeam wonders while giving Tom a clap on the back. "Do you need a cup of coffee…Water?" Shakeam offers.

"I'm afraid I won't be any good without something," Tom replies and when he tries to swallow it feels like a ball of cotton is caught in his throat.

Shakeam wonders what his good friend could be holding back and why. He is certain Tom is holding back pertinent information and Shakeam intends to pry it out of him.

Tom carefully contemplates his answer while watching the coffee drip into a paper cup. He'll certainly want to know where she can be reached, he reasons. His thoughts race off-the-board and tip-the-scales of logic until it occurs to him that the only solution is to lie.

Around the corner, Laura peeps out of her cubicle after hearing Tom's voice drifting from Shakeam's office. She notices him at Shakeam's espresso machine and is nearly knocked down by Shakeam who races past her in the hall. Tom is so engrossed in his thoughts he doesn't even notice her intruding upon his space and is startled by her soft alluring voice.

"Are you alright?" She looks back at Shakeam and slips into his office to talk with Tom. "I can't help but notice that you seem overly tense this morning."

He smiles at her ruefully, then, reaches for his hot coffee.

"I'm in sort-of-a-meeting right now," he explains and salutes her with the coffee before carefully taking a sip. "I'll come by when it's over," he promises.

She graciously nods and hurries back into the hall. "No problem. We'll talk later."

Shakeam returns to the office ready for an explanation about Cally's disappearance.

"Well!" he urges when Tom takes another careful sip of his coffee.

"Well, what?" Tom stalls and is taken aback by Shakeam's aggression.

"You know what I mean!" Shakeam snaps and bangs an angry fist down on his desk. Hot coffee spills and splashes all over the papers on his desk and speckles his white dress shirt. Tom grabs a handful of paper towels and dabs the coffee with them.

"I hate to have to tell you this, but she will be taking care of a sick Aunt for a while and didn't leave a forwarding address." Tom throws the ball back into Shakeam court. "I'm sure she'll call once she gets settled in."

"Did she give you a number?" he asks.

He feels awful about the cloud of despair drifting over Shakeam's face.

"Are you sure you have no way of contacting her?" he pleads.

"Nope!" Tom responds through a pucker, "No way! That's how she is. She disappears when she wants to and shows up when it's convenient. She doesn't know the meaning of commitment," Tom convinces.

Shakeam reluctantly accepts his friend's answer, even though it does put Cally in a quirky light.

Tom takes a moment to exhale and applauds himself for keeping his boss at-bay for a little while longer. Now that the aliens are gone, Tom intends to turn his undivided attention toward Laura.

CHAPTER 32

THE COUNCIL'S DECISION

The Aliens file, one-by-one, out of the spacecraft into the well-guarded Council member's chamber. They are simultaneously hoisted up, by a ray of fluorescent blue light, onto a platform suspended in mid-air. They cannot see the Council members since personal contact and knowledge of their identity is strictly forbidden. However, through the brightness of the light, the outline of a great multitude of celestial beings peering down on them, is clear.

"Let the questioning begin!" a thunderous voice bellows. Fear flows over them like great waves of the sea.

"What's the nature of these humans? Are they worthy of our intervention? Are they capable of defending themselves? Are they ready to be weaned from the confines of gravity? How fast are they evolving?" The rapid fire of questioning continued for hours.

Cally has a few answers she would like to keep to herself and is grateful for the ability to block most from probing her thoughts. If the Council could penetrate her thoughts now, they would discover she has succumbed to that human phenomenon known as love. Her thoughts are at the Council briefing, but somehow, her heart is still with Shakeam. The desire to be with him is suddenly overwhelming. She concludes that she must find a way to be with him again and hopes the Council will not attempt to stop her.

Myriads of voices echo from behind soft colorful spotlights randomly appearing before them in the true hues of a rainbow. The lights appear to dance before them throughout the entire questioning process. Yet, Cally and her associates remain calm in the face of the Council, without even blinking an eye at the most provocative questioning tactics. Finally, it all comes to an end and the stadium, full of spectators, anxiously waits to hear the verdict. Many anticipate the worst of Earth and have already come to terms with their demise.

"Let the answers begin!" a thunderous voice bellows.

Cally is the one selected by her associates to speak on their behalf. She stares into the soft illumination and steps forward.

"Respected Council, we find the earth still too primitive to stand alone," she states emphatically. Her argument in support of earth continues for the space of one hour. In the end, the Council decides unanimously to send a defense force to defend earth from the renegades of the galaxy. Then, the ambassadors retired to their homelands.

CHAPTER 33
PREHISTERIA

On Prehisteria, Frank and Terry settle back into their daily routines and even sign-up to participate in the yearly hunt of the Gorganauts. These are the small pesky creatures that pilfer the land in their cities and destroy their wild game.

As the hunts come to an end, onlookers wrestle among themselves to make their way to the front of the parade lines. All are anxious to cheer on their favorite hunter and to be seen by their opponents. Frank receives the Golden Hunter's Staff for killing more Gorganauts than anyone else in the recorded history of their games. He gives a victory speech, and most are astonished by his humility.

"Thank you all for this prestigious award. I owe my good fortune to the support of Terry, my spouse, and only true love." Frank says while holding his trophy high in the air.

Before he left for earth, he didn't have a humble bone in his body. He now reveals a side of his personality that no one on his planet has ever seen. All are somewhat perplexed, yet happy enough to continue celebrating the games. Humility is not encouraged among hunters in Prehisteria. Raw aggression is the most coveted emotion among men and women alike.

The choice women of his tribe perform a ceremonial dance in celebration of his great achievement. Terry blushes at the provocative way the females dance before her husband. They swerve from side-to-side, then, turn to bounce their generous breast against his. They repeat this ritual until Frank gets up and goes to the serving tables. There he gorges himself until morning or whenever the food runs out.

After the excitement of the games dies down, Terry invites all her children, grandchildren, and their offspring over for a sleepover. She enjoys the wide-eyed expressions on each face as she tells them all about her adventures on the other side of the galaxy. While she and Frank reminisce, their eyes meet and at that moment they both have a longing to return to planet earth. However, there are more games to be played on their home planet that cannot be ignored. As the lead hunter, all of Frank's tribesmen will expect him to lead them into the vast fields of prey.

Even so, Frank and Terry both agree that their work on earth is undone, and that Tom is still in need of their assistance. The hunts can wait, they conclude. The friends and relatives must make-do without them for a little while longer. They intend to find a way back to earth and find it soon.

CHAPTER 34
THE TRAITORS

G.W. secretly reports to the clandestine mutinous Sect within the Council as scheduled. He turns over all the information gathered pertaining to Earth. He intends to stick close to them to find out exactly what they intend to do with the data he gives them.

"This is perfect," the Sect leader tells a comrade. "We will invade planet earth and annihilate the weak humans!"

Before G. W. visited Earth, he didn't care whether the humans lived or died. Now that he has lived among them and gotten to know them as individuals, he has an overwhelming desire to go back to earth to ensure their safety. And although he has been sworn to secrecy by these dastardly space pirates, he feels it will be prudent to share this information with someone he can trust. Therefore, he confesses to Cally all he has heard and seen concerning the Sect and assures her he is an innocent pawn in his defense.

"I assure you, my Lady, I played the role of the fool in all of this treachery and-and-and" he stutters with the accent of a true southern Civil War officer. "I love the humans."

CALLY FEELS DUTY BOUND to report G. W.'s actions to Council members who meticulously review her report. They unanimously agree that humans are still mere infants within the whole scheme of things.

"The fact that they have made considerable progress over the past 100 years is noteworthy," comments the senior member. "For this reason, this species of people is worthy to be protected until further notice."

Therefore, the Council demands that all species allow humans to develop without further outside interference. Cheering rings throughout the stadium and many members stand to applaud the decision. However, the Sect members stand and turn their backs on the Council leaders.

"May I say one more thing, Honorable Council Leader?" Cally pleads.

"Have your say," the Council Leader tells her.

"There is an evil among the Council known as the Sect. I've been informed by a reliable source that they intend to destroy the inhabitants of Earth. They already have an army waiting someplace in this galaxy and they are prepared to destroy Earth now," she passionately tells them. "If you allow the Sect to continue, they will bring about genocide against every weaker species in existence. They must be stopped!" she pleads.

Various Council members cringe while she reveals the scrupulous intentions of their own colleagues. The Sect's intentions of joining hands with their enemies to gain the upper hand in the heavens, has been confirmed.

"You who have joined our enemies and have become enemies of our state must be condemned in the harshest way possible," she demands to a cheering audience. "I call for unity among our ranks once again and call for a purging of the universe!" she rouses.

The members roar and stomp feet, hands, arms, etc. in unison.

"You traitors will not leave this assembly today!" she shouts while holding up a piece of paper with the names of the traitors written on it. Certain Council members bolt for the exits and to their shame, they are quickly detained.

CHAPTER 35
GOING BACK

Another sleepless night has Cally turning the pages of the past. Shakeam appears to be the only topic on the pages. All she can think about is getting back to him. Whenever she does fall asleep, she wrestles over a recurring dream about Shakeam being engulfed in a fire inferno and screaming for help. The sleepless nights and the strong sense of danger are the driving force behind her desire to return to earth by any means necessary.

The spacecraft she just purchased is a far-cry from the one that carried her to Earth before. Nevertheless, she concludes, it will have to do. She has spent all her earnings plus borrowed bargaining chips to purchase it. Now, all she needs is a crew to help her pilot it all the way back to earth. The only crew members she believes can be trusted are her former associates. It doesn't take her long to convince them all the urgency to immediately return to planet Earth.

"No one knows better than I of the dangers of returning to earth. We were able to prevent certain Council members from revealing Earth's defense capabilities. Yet, they are still in danger of being invaded by forces outside of our galactic realm," she explains. "For this reason, we need to somehow alert them of the dangers they face ahead. Humans need to be shaken out of the stupor they appear to be in. We must make them prepare for war in the heavens," she explains with conviction.

Cally is certain that their going back is Earth's only real chance at survival. They must be saved from impending doom and destruction.

CHAPTER 36
ON THE ROAD AGAIN

On Jupiter, the cool air has Cally looking for something to sling over her bare arms. Cally has chosen to remain in the slinky human body she chose while on earth. This body is comfortable and reminds her of Tom and Shakeam—she doesn't intend to ever forget either of them.

The crew keeps a watchful eye on Cally as she checks the instruments. Being hopeful the used spacecraft will pass inspection; she calculates their distance from the weigh station to Earth and discovers they are halfway there.

The ship passes inspection, and they pack up to depart for Earth once again. The silence of her associates is puzzling. However, she doesn't bother to question them about it. They are all boarding the ship again and that's all that matters.

"We all need to be well-rested once we reach Earth," she reminds them. All agree without argument or debate, and this astonishes Cally even more. Even so, she flows with the moments of harmony and doesn't question them.

"I'll prepare the deep sleep chambers," she says, then, takes a deep breath. "G. W. will remain awake to watch over us while we rest."

She steps into the last sleep chamber programmed especially for her. Her body changes back into its original form just before she doses off to sleep. While asleep, she dreams of Shakeam and his proposal of marriage to her. "Yes, my dear," she whispers moments before her body finally yields to a deep peaceful rest.

THE END
Not Over

EARTHBOUND

THREE YEARS LATER

Korey bounces up and down on his parent's bed. He reaches the foot of it and tumbles backwards over the edge. At the blink of an eye, his 3-year-old frame rounds into a bouncing rubber ball.

"Okay Mommy," he yells to Cally, his mother, in the next room.

"Hum," she says aloud. "Sounds like Korey is bouncing off the walls again." Cally is continuously baffled by his supernatural abilities as well as her own. She carries the cell phone into the room where her son is bouncing from wall-to-wall in the form of a volleyball.

"Okay young man," she playfully tells him, then, attempts to catch her son in the middle of a bounce. "How many times do I have to warn you about doing that around here," she scolds. "What if your father were to walk in on you? You wouldn't want him to think you are strange, would you?" she reasons. In the blink of an eye, he changes back to human form.

"But Mommy," he whines. "Nobody knows, so, who cares."

She lifts him off the bed and high onto her shoulders. Then, she does a flying airplane to the doorway where she gently sets him down again.

"Shoos!" she orders and playfully smacks him on his bottom.

He waddles towards a stack of toys in the corner of the family room. "Let's go wash for dinner."

Cally is keenly aware that she and her son have a gift no one else appears to possess, at least, not among her circle of peers. When she gave birth to him while at home alone, the child simply oozed out of her like gelatin. She literally freaked and assumed it was her water breaking, until it became the solid form of a healthy crying baby boy right before her eyes. She was certain that something was seriously wrong, so she drove herself to a hospital emergency room. After she was examined, the Doctor was amazed that she healed so quickly. He complimented her on having good genes and walked towards the door until she leaped up from her bed and blocked his way.

"My baby!" she cries with trembling out-stretched hands. "He came out looking like orange gelatin!"

That certainly caught his attention. He examined the child who appeared to be in exceptional health too. Then, he ordered a heavy sedative for Cally and contacted Shakeam who cut a business trip short to be with her.

Ever since that night, he keeps a watchful eye on his wife and the baby. Shakeam downgraded his position to exclude all overnight business trips. And he no longer goes out once a week to play cards with his friends. She's not certain about all the Doctor may have said to Shakeam. Whatever was said though caused him to be overly protective of her and the baby from that moment on. He is afraid to venture farther away than his downtown office and stays at home every weekend.

Therefore, she's decided not to share the details surrounding the traffic accident she had days earlier:

> "Don't let go of the cart, baby," she instructs her little son while struggling to push the grocery cart over the slick snow-packed parking lot. The hole ahead was concealed by more falling snow causing the cart to tip over. When Korey falls into it, he goes down on one knee in front of an oncoming car which is unable to stop. She quickly changes into something huge, furry, and fierce. Immediately, she scoops Korey and the shopping cart out of the street and within a flash she assumes its feminine human form once again.

"Mommy, furry!" Her son laughs. Her transformation remains a blur and a mystery. She is certain that Shakeam would pay to send her to every doctor he could think of if he found this out.

"So, how was your day?" he calmly asked that night while handing her a hot cup of soothing tea.

"Good," she quickly responds while wondering whether Korey already spilled-the-beans about their day.

She senses suspicion all over him, and this suspicion is troubling her. She doesn't blame Shakeam. He has questions that she does not have the answers to. Such as: Who is she and why does she possess these supernatural abilities?

"Okay, I guess…it was sort of good," she confides with a hint of uncertainty in her voice.

Shakeam's hands slide over hers as they surround the warm cup. They tremble uncontrollably and his suspicions are confirmed. Shakeam is now certain that she is hiding something. And this something is too complicated for their young son to find the words to reveal.

Korey usually is excited about sharing every detail of his day with his father. On this day, however, he is tight-lipped about something. He is sullen and withdrawn and disappears into his room without even being told.

"So, tell me," He probes. "What happened today?"

After placing the cup of tea on the nightstand, she attempts to conceal the uneasiness she feels in the pit of her stomach.

"I don't recall exactly what took place," she stops to contemplate an appropriate response. "I mean…" she pauses, "One moment I was going across the parking lot, then the cart goes into a hole with our son in it. A car was headed directly for him, so I scooped him up and out of harm's way. I only don't recall rescuing him even though I must have.

He goes down on one knee…" she hesitates to weigh each word carefully. "I scoop him up into my arms and then, the next thing I know, I'm getting into the car and Korey's screaming his head off."

BLISSFUL UNION

The 2024 blizzard has left ice, laden with snow, on every exposed corner of the city of Denver. Tom is amazed by so many passer-byers who have dared to drive downtown today. Laura called him everything short of a fool for giving in to Shakeam's every demand and going to the office on a day like this. However, he's more than a boss to him, Tom reflects, Shakeam is a dear friend who has bailed him out in more ways than he cares to share with her. The cubicles lining the wall adjacent to his office are all empty. He guesses they'll be in later or not at all because of the forecast promising more snow. He intends to join them in the-land-of-snooze as soon as Shakeam is finished with him. "Must be important," he tells himself. He is startled to his feet by a faint knock at the door.

"Are you decent man?" Shakeam jokes while humbly entering Tom's domain. "I believe we're the only two here," he smiles then hands him one of two coffees.

Tom poises himself on one corner of his classic mahogany desk and takes a few welcoming sips of coffee. The seriousness of this meeting is written on the tension lines creasing Shakeam's forehead.

"So…" Tom asks with reservations. "What's going on?"

"I just have to confide in someone," he tells Tom through an uneasy grin. "You're like family, man," he nervously rubs both hands together. "And Cally and little Korey," he explains as his upper lip begins to quiver.

Tom braces himself to receive the worse news ever. He sits on the edge of his seat and patiently waits for Shakeam to toss him the news.

Shakeam is touched by Tom's concern and begins to reveal all the strange things Cally has been saying and doing.

"She forgets things, you know what I mean," he tells Tom.

"Not really," Tom responds.

"She falls and forgets how she got there. The baby cries and she doesn't know why because she claims she blanks everything out," he confides. "Ever since Korey was born, her doctor advised me to keep an eye on her because he suspects she's been hallucinating."

"No, that can't be. This doesn't sound like the Cally I know," Tom empathizes with both Shakeam and Cally, but he's not able to reveal what he knows.

"I know, right. She was always so sharp and sure of herself before Korey came along," he recalls.

"Don't worry. We'll get to the bottom of this," Tom assures him.

Shakeam gives him a pat on the back. "I hoped you'd see this as a team effort. I don't think I can cope with this on my own."

"So, tell me my friend," he asks. "How is it that your cousin never heard of skiing, football, basketball, or any other American national pastime?" Shakeam instinctively reaches for the granite paper weight on Tom's desk. He lifts it towards himself then down again, treating it like a small exercise bell.

Suddenly, Tom is under fire. The questions have his head spinning. He has the answers, but these answers must remain secret.

"Look," Tom tells him and says, "I know she appears to be a little odd at times--" he pauses for the right words. "But she means well, and the bottom line is this," he says while pushing away from his desk and standing to his feet. "Does she love you and do you genuinely love her?"

Shakeam is conscious of the fact that he can only answer that question in the affirmative. Of course, he loves her and is certain that she loves him. His questioning does not involve love. He wonders whether she is sane or not. He decides to let the conversation end right where it is. However, he has decided to continue it after gathering more concrete evidence about the matter.

"That's it," he tells Tom. "No more questions, for now."

"I know you'll give me the answer sooner or later," Shakeam says with confidence while they stroll towards the door.

"What do you mean by that," wonders Tom.

"It's always about the love!" Shakeam nods while raising his hand to receive a high-five.

Back at home, Tom adjusts logs in the fireplace while Laura showers. It has been a long hard day and Tom rejoices when the twins finally bed down for the night. Aylia, Laura's daughter, has also temporarily left the nest, by attending a sleepover at a friend's home.

Tom and Laura have been married for three years now. She gave birth to their twin boys eight months ago, so their spare time has become a precious commodity.

Finally, we're alone, he thinks while pouring wine into two long-stemmed wine glasses. He sets the glasses on the coffee table and dims the lights. Then, he opens the curtains leading to their spacious patio. White fluffy snowflakes float down from a royal blue sky and Tom is in awe by their magical beauty. Satisfied that his mission to create an ambience of romance is complete, he stretches out on their soft sofa and waits for Laura to return. Memories of their fairytale romance bring a wide smile to Tom's face while replacing her fallen hero has been his greatest fear. He is not a replacement in her eyes, but a welcome addition to her life. Proof of this came to light at their wedding, where everyone received him with open arms, including her parents.

Laura takes a deep breath while entering the room and finds her faithful husband resting on the sofa. She clears her throat which causes him to open his eyes and peer up at her. He must be dreaming about heaven, he thinks, while Laura stands over him adorned in a fuchsia T-strapped Victoria Secret nighty. He wraps both arms around her and draws her close to him. She loses her balance and falls on top of his warm body.

"I knew there was something I liked about these blizzards," he whispers and begins nibbling on one ear.

LOST MEMORIES

Frank and Terry have no recollection of a battle taking place in their Galaxy. However, rumor has it that a fierce battle did take place. They don't recall entering their ship to return home and no one around them ever mentions them leaving home for a second excursion. Three years ago, they both woke up in bed without any memory of how they got there. The events that took place on Earth during their second visit have all disappeared. News of the war came from friends and family members and the two of them never let on that they were oblivious to those past events. They enjoy being treated like heroes on their home planet, however, up until this very moment, it never occurs to them to ask why. They've escaped annihilation along with the rest of the galaxy. Everyone appears to be happy about the outcome, so, they are happy too.

After three long years, Terry heard a rumor about the whereabouts of Cally. She tells Frank that Cally is living on planet earth as a human. He doesn't want to believe it and vows to catch a transport to Earth to see if it's true for himself.

"If you go, I'm going too," Terry promises. "I didn't care for her in the beginning," she confesses. "Even so, we became a dynamite team. I miss her."

Frank wraps his arms around her. "I miss her too. We must find out what's going on. We must know."

While on planet earth, Cally is beginning to recall the carefree lifestyle of her previous existence. Even though her excursions with her associates were testy at times, she enjoyed the adrenaline rush their adventures gave her. Yes, she does recall their adventures together, however, she doesn't know why she initially came to Earth.

"I bet Frank and Terry are up to their necks in trouble right now," she smiles and conceals it the moment Shakeam enters the room.

"What? Did you say something Dear?" he asks while passing through on the way to the kitchen.

"Oh no, Sweetheart," she replies. "--Just talking to myself again."

If only I knew what I was up against, she thinks. Who am I? She wonders. She asks herself about the outcome of the mission and is certain that she is on Earth for the purpose of a mission. I believe Tom has the answers to my dilemma. He must reveal it willingly or she is determined to get the information she desires by utilizing her abilities.

In the meantime, Tom is content with being the husband of Laura and the proud father of twins. He's not concerned with the affairs of the Galactic Council any longer. Every now and then, he recalls the excitement of the adventures he and the Aliens had. Nevertheless, he has decided to obey the wishes of the Council members which is to forget it all ever happened. The fireworks in the sky never came to Earth and the experts said they were all the results of meteor showers. So, he's not certain about all that took place in the heavens, he only knows that he did his part, which was to be an ambassador for the planet earth.

EPILOGUE 4
G. W. CARVER'S ON PLUTONIUM

Far, far away, beyond the Milky Way and the known Universes, G. W. Carver resides on planet Plutonium.

"Is he awake?" G. W. Carver hears someone ask.

"He's moving," the other person says.

G. W. Carver jumps to his feet and finds himself faced with two Jovials, normally found on the planet Plutonium, which is the farthest known planet away from the Council.

"Where am I?" he huffs.

The Jovials look puzzled. The filthiness of their appearance and the stench coming from them disgust G. W. Carver.

"Don't you know?" one of them asks.

"We're your best friends," the other replies.

"We're your only friends," they both laugh.

G. W. Carver senses they are both telling the truth, yet he has no recollection of them. He does, however, vividly remember the war and being separated from his team of travelers.

"What year is this?" he wants to know.

"Well, I don't know, but we've been together for three lunar years," one of them tells him.

"This can't be," he protests. "Where are Cally and the rest of my friends? What happened to Tom? And, most importantly—what happened to Earth?"

———————

THE END

www.ingramcontent.com/pod-product-compliance
Lightning Source LLC
Chambersburg PA
CBHW030004010826
48973CB00009B/2655